D0898000

First Orchid
for Pat

First Orchid for Pat

---

by ANNE EMERY

Philadelphia
THE WESTMINSTER PRESS

First Orchid
for Pat

1

When Pat Marlowe became engaged to Tim Davis, she was a junior in high school, he was a senior, and the future looked far, far away. It was enough to be in love, to talk daily on the telephone, to spend all their time together, and to plan for that faraway future.

But now all of a sudden the long satisfying summer was past, Tim was leaving for college tomorrow, early, and she was only a high school girl being left behind alone. Tears of protest filled her eyes and she thought she could not bear the separation, especially with Tim talking so reasonably about each seeing other people during the coming year to be sure they were making no mistake about each other.

" So we'll trade bracelets back again and break up," Pat said, keeping her voice steady with an effort. " That ought to please everyone."

She took the heavy silver bracelet off her wrist where she had worn it day and night for almost four months and handed it to him.

" But it doesn't mean anything," Tim assured her, holding her close. " We're only being reasonable, honey. I couldn't stand it to think of your not having any fun all

7

this year. And our folks think we ought to test it out for a year to make sure how we really feel. I know and you know. But they don't."

"Oh, sure," Pat said drearily, not agreeing at all, but accepting a situation that could not be changed. "We're too young, there's so much time ahead, how do we know what we want? — and all the rest of it. I've heard it a million times." Her voice broke on the ageless protest, "They don't understand; they don't even remember what it's like!"

They sat in the car, looking over the quiet lake with the silver ribbon of moonlight accenting the unbroken surface of the dark water, and she looked at Tim again, feeling as if the end of the world would come when he left for Crandall College. His lean profile was strong in the moonlight, his black hair curved away from his forehead, and his eyes looked as if they had been arranged to smile. She missed the heavy bracelet already; she felt as if she had been cut adrift without it.

"Well, let's go home and tell your folks the good news," he said. "They'll probably be glad to hear about it."

If her mother betrayed any pleasure over this "breaking up," Pat thought, she would never tell her another thing. Tim kissed her in another promise that in thus pleasing their parents nothing would be changed, and turned the car toward home, while Pat stared out of the window, looking into the dark maze of time to come. She would go out with other boys, Tim would go out with other girls, the hussies, and at the end of the year they would be together again. But the year looked so long that she was terrified. Anything could happen in a year, she thought, trying not to believe it.

8

When Tim was gone, Pat alternated between depression and a fine creditable attitude of cheerful resignation. Part of the intermittent cheerfulness was due to the other romance in her family in which Pat took almost as much interest as in her own. Her brother, Mike, leaving for Princeton the day after Tim left for Crandall, was dejected about leaving Connie Reid.

Connie had been Pat's best friend for years now. The Reids lived around the corner from the Marlowes, and Connie had admired Mike since she had been twelve years old. Not until last spring had Mike recognized Connie's special charms, and when he took her to the senior prom in June, Pat had felt that truly love conquered all. She could understand why Mike was unhappy these last days, and she undertook to encourage him as Tim had encouraged her.

"But it's altogether different," Mike said with a touch of impatience at the idea that there could be any similarity between the two affairs. "You're nuts about Tim. But Connie isn't nuts about me. That's the whole trouble."

"Oh, she is too," Pat spoke confidently. "Why, she's been crazy about you for years! "

"Hah! " Mike exploded dourly. "If a girl really likes you, she'll go steady, won't she? And Connie won't. So what does that prove? "

He was packing as he talked, and he slammed half a dozen folded shirts into his trunk and had to take them all out and refold them.

"Tim and I aren't going to go steady this year," Pat said, eager to review her own situation and reinforce her own confidence. "We both feel we ought to go out with other people while we're separated. But it isn't going to mean a thing, really."

9

"That's what you think," Mike muttered. "Suppose old Tim finds some campus queen and never comes back?"

That was the very supposition that turned Pat cold whenever she thought of it, and it was chilling to have it come from someone else as if it were entirely possible.

She was silent a moment and then she said bravely, "But that can't happen because Tim and I are seriously in love."

Mike said, "Hah!" again, but he made no further effort to discourage her. The telephone rang, and he leaped to answer it before Pat could move.

"Hi, honey." His voice was warm and soft and it reminded Pat painfully of Tim. "Why, sure. I'm nearly packed. Now, I'm writing every day, so be sure you've got a good supply of stationery on hand. I'll be awful lonesome 'way off there." The conversation went on for several minutes, and Pat, feeling that it was sickeningly cooing, went on down to find her mother and check on the final arrangements for seeing Mike off.

"Denny is going along tomorrow," Mrs. Marlowe said. "Are you going with us?"

"Why, I guess so," Pat said. "I haven't anything else to do now that Tim's gone. Is Connie going?"

"I don't know if there will be room," Mrs. Marlowe said. "There'll be five of us as it is."

But Connie had other plans and could not go anyway, and Mike was sunk in gloom.

However, Connie appeared as they were loading the car on Sunday afternoon to leave for the station.

"Why, I wouldn't let you leave for college without saying good-by," she reproached him. "Now cheer up, Mike. You'll have a wonderful time, and Princeton is going to be

10

lucky to get you on the football team."

"Sounds good," Mike muttered, trying not to let his pleasure show, "but they've got some good players and I'm only a freshman this year."

"I'd give anything if I could see you play," Connie mourned vivaciously. "Don't they have a prom or something following a game, where the girls get a chance to see the whole show?"

He brightened a little. "They probably do. I want you to come for all the dances anyway."

His mother remarked casually, inspecting the baggage before she told him to close the trunk of the car: "Of course Connie will want to come to Princeton while you're there. But it's a long way, and a lot of carfare for a date every weekend."

There was a dull silence, while everyone tried to think of something cheerful to say. Why did adults have to chill every bright idea like that? Pat wondered, in a kind of desperate frustration. After all, Mike would have found out, Connie would have found out — they didn't have to be told. They were only making chatter to cheer up this moment of separation.

"Oh, well," said Mike, trying for a cheerful alternative, "I could always transfer back here if Princeton is too far away."

The Marlowes climbed into the car, making no response to this future possibility.

"I think I left my wallet," Mike muttered. "You wait here while I go in and hunt around. Want to come with me, Connie?"

They walked hand in hand up the steps and into the house, and Pat sat beside Denny in the back seat of the car, waiting. Eleven-year-old Denny was sober today, as if it took concentrated effort to digest the importance of his big brother's departure for college.

He sat up after a few minutes and scowled at the house.

"What's taking them so long anyway?" he demanded. "Mike's wallet was right on the hall table. I saw it."

"How's your new teacher?" Pat asked quickly. "How does it feel to be in sixth grade?"

"Aw, it's O.K." Denny, diverted from his complaint, relapsed again into thoughtful silence.

Mrs. Marlowe, next to her husband at the wheel, was looking out of the window toward the street, and Pat was hoping she would say nothing about Mike and Connie going into the house together. After all, a boy could not say good-by to his best girl properly in front of his mother and father, out on the street in the middle of Sunday afternoon.

"I simply couldn't stand it if he transferred back here," Mrs. Marlowe said with quiet violence. "When I think of having to watch him play football another four years and get carried off the field in every other game — well, I couldn't stand it, that's all. And how he can even think of leaving Princeton — he must be out of his head! I won't have him home, that's final."

"Don't get excited," her husband soothed her. "He probably doesn't mean it, anyway."

"Life would be so much simpler without love," said Mrs. Marlowe.

Pat smiled to herself. "Simple, yes. But look how dull."

"I could enjoy a dull life for a few years. Aren't those kids ever coming back? It's time to leave."

Mike and Connie reappeared before she touched the

horn ring, and Connie said, as they approached the car, "Have a wonderful year, Mike, and keep writing."

He stopped and looked down at her, oblivious of witnesses.

"You be sure to answer; that's all I want."

Denny watched them with scornful indifference, but refrained from comment.

"So long — have fun, but not too much!" Mike said, with a forced smile. He climbed into the car with Pat and Denny. Connie stood watching as they drove away. When Pat looked back, she was touching her eyes and blowing her nose. But she smiled resolutely and waved until they turned a corner and she was out of sight.

"Well, on our way at last," said Mrs. Marlowe, with a sigh of relief. "Have you got your ticket, Mike? And your money?"

"Yeah, yeah, I've got everything," he said patiently. "Don't worry, Mom. Your little boy is going to get along all right."

He said no more all the way down to Chicago.

Funny, Pat thought, watching the traffic flow past them, how gloomy it was to send someone off to college. A boy was going off on his own for the first time, riding into adventure, facing a new life opening before him, and all his mother could think of was how much she was going to miss her boy, and Mike certainly did not look eager about his big step.

Maybe Mike would meet someone else, Pat thought, and it would serve Connie right. But she did not pursue that thought very far, because the same worry about Tim seemed to overhang it like a black cloud.

They parked the car and followed a porter into the train

13

shed and down the length of the long train. Pat's feet began to hurt from so much walking in heels.

"You've got a good Pullman seat," observed Mr. Marlowe with satisfaction, as he counted the bags and tipped the porter. "Well, son, these will be the best four years of your life. Don't waste time. Have fun, and write once in a while."

"Oh, sure, Dad," Mike replied. "Everything is going to be fine. Don't worry. I'll tell you all about everything after I get settled. Good-by, Mom." He kissed her lightly on the cheek. "Denny, good-by, boy! Take care of the folks." He winked at his small brother, who turned away embarrassed at all the sentiment attached to leave-taking. "And Pat, take care of yourself. And look after Connie. Don't let her get too lonesome."

"Don't worry," said Pat, trying not to sound satirical. Privately she did not think Connie was going to be nearly lonesome enough. The boy across the aisle from Mike was very attractive, she noticed, and she wondered if possibly he might be going to Princeton too.

It was time to leave the train, and they stood on the platform waving good-by as the train pulled away. Mike looked cheerful behind the window and a little self-conscious about his parents' enthusiastic farewells. Pat stood on tiptoe, trying to see the boy on the other side of the aisle, and then, to her embarrassment, he was peering out of Mike's window and waving to people who seemed to be standing right next to the Marlowes. Pat was thankful she had said nothing aloud about him, as she would probably have done a year ago. She glanced at the boy's parents and noted that they looked just like parents: middle-aged, well-dressed, pleased that their son was going east to school, relieved that he was at last on the train. The boy had already made friends with Mike, and they were grinning at each other as if each recognized a parent problem for the other.

And then the train was gone. The Marlowes stood a moment looking at each other with that final recognition of separation in the family.

"I want an ice-cream cone." Denny had located the soda fountain. Pat gave him a dime to save discussion.

"Well, Mike is on his own now, and you're not going to worry about him, are you, Jo?" Mr. Marlowe turned toward the station exit.

"Not me," denied Mrs. Marlowe. "I'm so relieved to have him on his way. Only it does take a little getting used to, doesn't it?"

"Oh, sure, sure," agreed her husband, taking her arm. "But you'll have plenty on your mind this year. After all, you've still got Pat and Denny —"

Mrs. Marlowe laughed. "I'll have lots to think about."

"If Connie doesn't write every day, I'll kill her," Pat muttered. "I don't see how she can be so fickle."

Her mother discreetly said nothing. They drove back to Allandale with a growing sense of relief and exhilaration.

"So that begins the college year," she said to Pat, "and now you can really settle down to being a senior."

"Well, it is fun to be with the kids again," Pat said broodingly. "But with only a couple of weeks past it already seems like such a long year. In fact, I hate being a senior: no one ahead of me, no one older than I am. I can hardly wait till I'm in college where there'll be some older men again."

15

2

Although school had opened before Mike's departure for college, summer was not yet over, and the weather was hot and sticky. Everyone on the bus was complaining about having to be in school when the day was just right for swimming or at least for dressing in hot-weather clothes like shorts and sandals. But under the complaints Pat could sense the anticipation she herself felt.

She wore a pink-and-white checked gingham dress that Tim had liked on summer-night dates.

"It makes you look like a baby doll," he had told her tenderly.

Now, watching the boys drift through the bus and collect together at the back, watching the girls eying the boys, noticing the couples who got on together, Pat wished she had not worn the pink-and-white gingham. It reminded her too much of Tim.

But today everything reminded her of Tim. She had a locker in the same location as last year, and as she opened it she remembered how Tim had always appeared beside her before the morning began, and how he had met her there every night before she left for home. She had given him the combination of her lock, and he kept some of his own books there and brought hers to her when she had been absent. She had loved sharing the locker with him, and clanging it open, she felt like a widow, she told herself.

"It feels funny to be alone in a locker after the way Tim used it last year," she remarked to Connie, who was next to her.

"Probably," said Connie with a little smile, as if she were thinking of something amusing. "But there are some advantages in being alone, don't forget."

Did that mean that she was looking forward to Mike's being away all year? Pat wondered, her mind jumping at once to Mike's defense.

"When you've gone steady as long as Tim and I have, it takes a while to discover those advantages," she remarked.

Connie shrugged. She was a slim, brown-haired girl with a pretty figure and since last spring she had gained a great deal of poise and assurance. Now she hoisted an armload of books into place and turned toward her home room, halfway down the hall. She walked like a model, Pat thought, with the envy that she frequently felt when she looked at Connie. Pat raised her own books a little higher, lifted her head, threw her shoulders back, and took smaller steps with her ankles together. She was a senior now, one of the grown-up group, and independent. And although she missed last year's seniors, already she enjoyed the aura of being a senior herself more than she had anticipated.

"Hi, Bob!" she cried as a plump red-haired boy went past smiling cordially. "Abby! How are you! Hi, there!"

17

She had forgotten how many people she knew and liked, and without Tim to take all her attention she was glad to be with them again. Senior year could be fun, after all. She turned into her home room, feeling that she was back in the old routine almost as if there had never been a break in it.

The "big crowd" was as important as ever, the Y Club girls as friendly and busy as last year, Connie was alone as she had been before she began going with Mike last spring — nothing had changed, except that Tim was no longer around. And as the day went by, Pat missed him more and more. This freedom that Connie commended, what did you do with it?

During the lunch hour, Pat hunted out some of the other senior girls bereft of college-bound boy friends, and there was a bittersweet satisfaction in dwelling with each other on their lonely positions. Pat alternated between a sense of freedom and a sense of loss that seemed to attack her at unexpected moments. By three o'clock she could hardly wait to get home to see if there was a letter from Tim.

She and Connie went home together; it would be easier to face disappointment if she had company. And there were two letters. One had been mailed at eleven thirty, Saturday night, one yesterday at noon. Pat tore them open with trembling fingers.

"Oh, my poor baby," she breathed. "He's so homesick, Connie! Listen to this: 'There's nothing to do around here, and so far I haven't met any girls or anyone to talk to except my roommate. Dick is O.K., I guess, but his girl lives right in town here, and he's off with her most of the time. It sure makes me feel far away from mine — I miss you so much —'"

She laid that one down and picked up the other. "'Classes start tomorrow, and I think they're going to be good. But until then there's nothing to do around here, and I mean *nothing*. I did meet a nice guy this afternoon, and we're going to the town's one movie tonight.'

"I'm glad he's found someone to run around with," Pat continued to Connie. "Tim doesn't like everybody, and it isn't easy for him to get started in a new place. I worry about him so. I knew he'd be miserable at first."

She stuffed the letters into her schoolbooks, feeling as if a gap in her life had been closed.

"Come on out in the kitchen and let's find something to eat."

But all the time Pat was fixing tall glasses of Coke and ice and hunting for some cookies, she was disturbed about Tim's homesickness. She hoped freshman activities would begin soon, that he would find more people he would like and places to go, because what if he found a girl to console him while he felt like this?

To Connie she said, "Did you and Mike have any understanding about dating while he's away?"

"I told Mike he couldn't expect me to sit home and wait till he got back," Connie said. "I wouldn't expect him to sit around uselessly in the evenings, either. Did I tell you I met a new boy today in my French class?"

Her eyes sparkled, and her face lighted. Pat picked up the empty glasses with a sense of profound disgust. How anyone could be so fickle and unfeeling, she would never understand!

She wrote Tim a long letter that night, sympathizing, scolding, encouraging, and urging him to make more friends. She could hardly wait for him to come home, she

19

told him at the end. School seemed empty without him, and scarcely anything seemed worth-while.

She felt sure that the year was going to be equally unhappy for both of them. But when she mentioned this conviction to her mother, Mrs. Marlowe said, without any understanding at all, Pat felt, that life was like that: there would be many occasions when she would have to wait for time to pass, and meanwhile there were constructive things for which she could use it.

But her mother had never been through a separation like this, Pat was sure as she read and reread Tim's homesick letters. She wanted him so badly; she wanted to comfort him; she didn't see how she could stand this separation for a whole year; she couldn't bear for him to be so unhappy.

It was a shock, when ten days had gone by, to get a letter that was suddenly cheerful. Tim had gone to a freshman party on Saturday night and had met some students he had not known before. He had met a girl named Gwen, who was fun. He was beginning to feel as if he belonged at school, he was going to have more fun from now on, and it was not a bad place at all. He still loved Pat and could hardly wait to see her. But Crandall was pretty good.

There was only one letter that day, and the tone of solid cheer and contentment disturbed Pat more than the earlier letters had. Gwen must be a threat, she was convinced, an attractive girl whom he liked. And here Pat was, hundreds of miles away, and it was all too likely that she would never see him again. What if that girl asked him to her home for Thanksgiving and Christmas? What if he wanted to go? She was distraught with worry and she talked to her mother, driven by a need to find reassurance

20

from someone who ought to know.

"Now, honey, this is a very natural and logical thing," Mrs. Marlowe advised her distracted daughter. "Tim can't live like a hermit at school just because he was devoted to you."

"He's still devoted," Pat protested, feeling that the oftener she made the statement the truer it became. "He says so in every letter. I know he wouldn't change."

"Let him alone," her mother said firmly. "Don't try to tie a string to him. Tell him you're delighted he's having such a good time, and encourage him to tell you what he's doing. When he begins not saying anything, that will be the time to worry. But as long as he's writing every day, take it easy and be calm. How does he know you haven't found someone here at home to take his place?"

"But that's not the same thing at all!" Pat cried.

She blushed as she said it, knowing that it was exactly the same thing and that her own school life had suddenly picked up new interest. A boy in her history class had asked her to go to the football kickoff dance on the last Saturday in September, and although Pat cared little for the boy, still it was a chance to go to an important dance.

But more important than that, Jack Willis, who was in her English class, had begun walking through the hall with her occasionally, and had talked persuasively about her trying out for the play next week. Pat had always been interested in the dramatic productions, but last year she had not gone out for any of the plays, because Tim cared nothing for dramatics, and she preferred to give all her time to Tim. Jack's suggestion was stimulating, since being in dramatics would be something entirely different from anything she had ever done with Tim, and it would be an

21

activity she knew she would enjoy.

More than that, Jack was a member of the " big crowd," that important group whose activities Pat had observed from afar these three years past with interest and some envy. It was flattering to be noticed by a member of that distinguished group, and it was an opening, a chance, perhaps, to become part of a group she had never been able to join.

For the first time since school had opened she felt, with almost a sense of guilt, that it was an advantage to be free. Who knew what excitement lay ahead in her senior year?

3

Outside the windows of the English classroom, the western sun glared hot and full against the drawn shades. Inside the room the air was still and heavy, and Mr. Loomis' voice went on and on in a drone that seemed to flow thickly through the dense heat. As he talked, he kept mopping his forehead and under his chin with a folded handkerchief, and Pat felt sorry for him. Around her, students were lounging at their desks, tapping fingers noiselessly, rattling pencils, yawning helplessly. Pat intended to pay close attention to her teachers this year, to get top grades in every course. With college coming up, it was important to make a strong finish at Allandale High School. But the effort today was hopeless. She yawned in spite of herself and looked away from Mr. Loomis quickly, hoping he hadn't seen her.

Across the room Jack Willis was studying a notice on the blackboard, clowning in pantomime as he stared at it. He squinted his eyes, craned his head forward, rubbed his eyes, and took off imaginary spectacles, which he blew upon, rubbed carefully with an imaginary handkerchief, and replaced, fitting curved wire bows over his ears with meticulous care. Then he propped his chin on his hand and stared at the board long and thoughtfully, frowning in concentration, and at last he seemed to understand the words he read. Snapping his fingers, silently joyous, he nodded his comprehension, smiled widely, covered his mouth, and conquered imaginary hysterics of laughter.

Fascinated, Pat looked from him to the blackboard to see if there was really anything so funny as he implied. The notice on the board said, " Bring Holloway's *Readings in English Literature* tomorrow."

She looked back at Jack, whose amusement was subsiding, and he glanced at her as if he had expected her to notice him. She smiled to let him know she thought he was highly entertaining, and he bowed modestly in thanks and turned his attention back to Mr. Loomis as if he were conferring a favor upon the teacher.

When Pat looked at the teacher, she was sorry for him. She knew from his uneasy expression that he had been aware of Jack's antics and was not sure how to deal with him. Mr. Loomis went on talking, with nervous gestures, about the senior English program and how he hoped that when they had finished the year they would all have found some new interest in English literature beyond anything they had brought with them from the junior course. She wished the bell would ring.

Suddenly the classroom darkened. The sun had disappeared, and the heat remaining in the classroom was charged with suspense.

Jack Willis rose with conspicuous gallantry and raised one of the shades while Mr. Loomis watched him, suddenly silent.

" It seemed dark all of a sudden," Jack explained with a charming smile.

"Raise them all, if the sun is under a cloud," Mr. Loomis agreed.

The western sky was black with thunderheads, and forks of lightening streaked across the gloom. A terrific crash of thunder split the heat, and one of the girls shrieked. When the others looked at her in amusement she explained in coquettish excitement, "I've always been afraid of thunder, ever since I was a baby."

The class laughed in an explosion of relief at the change in the weather, the cessation of Mr. Loomis' long explanation, and Jack's pantomime of terror at the lightning flashes. Mr. Loomis sat at his desk, looking undecided whether he should try to pull the class together against the competing elements of weather and entertainment, or give up and laugh at Jack with the students.

To Pat's relief the bell rang, cutting off the comedy with an authoritarian peal. Everyone caught up books and papers and streamed into the hall in indecorous haste, chatting about the storm.

"How's your boy friend?" Jack Willis asked, at Pat's elbow, and she turned to smile at him.

"Oh, fine," she told him vivaciously. "He's beginning to have fun at Crandall. But I miss him so I'll be glad when he can come home for a weekend. How are you getting along?"

"So-so," he shrugged. He was tall and blond and slender, popular with the "big crowd," many of who, Pat noticed with pride, now spoke to her with an interest they had never shown before Jack Willis began walking from class to class with her. "Say, did you see the dates for the tryouts for *Good Housekeeping?*"

"I saw something about it in the school *Bulletin* this

25

morning." She tried to remember the details.

"Next week — Monday, Tuesday, Wednesday, and Thursday afternoons. You're coming out for it, aren't you?"

"I'm planning to," Pat said. "I don't know whether it will be worth-while or not. I always wanted to be in a school play, but last year I couldn't seem to find time."

"It'll be worth-while," he promised. "They always give seniors special consideration. And it's fun. I go out for all the dramatic productions, so I know." He stopped at the intersection where their ways parted and looked down at her. "I'll take you home this afternoon," he said. "This rain is pretty hard."

When she met him in the parking lot, grateful that she didn't have to stand on a corner in the downpouring rain, she noticed a red convertible streaking toward the exit.

"That car looks familiar," she gestured toward the convertible. "Whose is it?"

"The red Chevy?" He adjusted his rear-vision mirror, which she had bumped as she got in, and looked over his shoulder for traffic, rolling into the traffic lane away from the loading platform. "That's Nan's car. You know Nan Cameron, don't you?"

"I know who she is," Pat said. "We've never been in class together though, and she doesn't know me from a doorknob."

"I wouldn't be so sure about that," he reassured her. "I think she knows you." He sounded as if he knew what he was talking about, and Pat's mouth fell open. "I went steady with her for two years." He was swinging his car into the main road as he spoke, and his eyes were fixed on the traffic. "She's a swell kid, in fact, she's great. I guess

26

it was all my fault we broke up, and if I could fix things up, there's nothing I'd like better."

He had lapsed into gloom, and Pat glanced at him with interest, her mind immediately turning over possibilities for helping him to mend his broken romance. "What happened?"

He shrugged, implying the hand of inevitable fate.

"The usual thing, I guess. I was a camp counselor, so I was away all summer, and she went out to Nantucket with her folks in August. I guess she hit the local yokels pretty hard. Anyway, they gave her a big whirl, and I got jealous. That's all."

"But you shouldn't be jealous of something like that!" Pat cried. "Just a summer diversion — it didn't mean a thing. Why, Jack, you didn't break up over a silly thing like that, did you?"

"It was enough diversion that she didn't write more than once a week the whole month," he said, beginning to get angry again. "And her letters were full of all those boys with sailboats and yachts. She never even mentioned missing me or thinking of me."

"But she must have been thinking of you to write letters. So then?"

"I couldn't even date someone to get even," he muttered, "stuck away in camp like that. All I could do was get steamed up. I got so mad after one letter that I wrote and told her off and said if that was the way she wanted to spend her time when I was out of sight and out of mind, maybe I'd better stay out of sight. Then she got mad and said that was all right with her. Naturally I wrote right back that maybe I was hasty and anyway I didn't mean a word of it. But she wrote a long, understanding letter

27

about how she was afraid I meant even more than I said, and maybe we'd been seeing too much of each other for too long. Anyway, Roger was going to Yale in the fall and he'd already invited her to the first dance, so maybe we'd better let bygones be bygones and not complicate things again, that she'd always be a friend, and so on."

"But didn't you ask her for a date to get things straightened out when you were both back in town?" Pat demanded.

He nodded. "Oh, sure. When I called her she'd been home for three days, and the first I knew of it was when I saw her running around in her car. She said she didn't think I'd wanted to hear from her. And she was terribly sorry but she was busy three times in a row when I asked for dates — and then I got mad again. After all, a guy has to have some pride. I said as sweetly as possible that when she wanted to see me she could let me know — and she never has."

"No, I don't suppose she would." This sounded more complex and serious than Pat had thought at first. "The best thing you can do," she advised him, "is to find another girl. Get someone else you can take an interest in and talk to. In the first place, it's comforting, and in the second place, it will take your mind off Nan. And in the third place, it might get her interested all over again. Sometimes it works that way."

"You think so?"

"There's a good chance."

"Well, now," he said, grinning at her, "it might not be so hard at that to get interested in somebody else."

She laughed. "You flatter me. But don't get too much interested. I like you too much to break your heart and I'm

28

already involved. You know about Tim."

"Oh, sure," he said. "But out of sight, out of mind, don't you know? Anyway we can have fun, can't we?"

"Fun, yes."

It was fun to go out with Jack. He talked about Nan, and Pat talked about Tim, and each felt consoled about his own problems. Jack answered Pat's questions with straightforward masculine understanding that left her more knowledgeable about how men felt about things. Sometimes he put on an act designed to make the student body think they were madly in love with each other and afterward, when he and Pat were alone, he was convulsed with laughter at his own humor. And so long as Pat did not want him to be serious, it was delightful to laugh.

In many ways he filled Tim's place at high school, and the ache disappeared, which made Pat feel that she was becoming very mature about adapting herself to his absence. When Tim wrote about Gwen, with whom he was spending a lot of time, Pat could talk to Jack about it and find comfort in his explanation that it meant nothing.

But more than anything else, she appreciated his pulling her into the dramatic activity of the school, something that had no connection with Tim, hence reminding her of no happy memories, and something that promised to fill her time full enough to make it pass quickly.

4

She met Jack for the Monday afternoon tryout and found a pleasant satisfaction in walking into the auditorium with him in full sight of the "big crowd." She waved to Connie and half a dozen others she knew. Jack nodded to Nan as if he barely knew her, and Pat noticed that Nan's mobile, piquant face showed lively curiosity about his companion. But she smiled at Pat in a friendly way. She looks as if she'd be fun to know, Pat thought.

The lead in the play, announced at the end of the week, went to Nan Cameron, who was slim and dark and talented. One of the minor parts went to Jack. And Pat, hoping against odds that she might get into the play, was enchanted to get a small part.

The play was becoming a turning point in her life, Pat began to think a couple of weeks later. At first she was pleased and flattered when the director, Mr. Jennings, told her, "Very good, Pat!" with a lift of surprise in his voice as if, she thought, he might have given her the lead, if only he had realized earlier how good she was. She noticed the skill of the other players. Connie, she thought with objective decision, was not really gifted at all. However, it was evident that Connie did not know the difference and was well pleased with her own performance. Nan was very, very good, Pat decided, still being entirely objective. She liked Nan very much, off the stage as well as on.

If it had not been for the play, she might never have had a chance to know Nan like this, and Nan Cameron was rapidly becoming one of her best friends. Jack's own part was so small that he did not have to be present at all the rehearsals. But Pat couldn't stay away. Whether she was called for rehearsal or not, she loved every minute of work on the play. Nan was always there, and when Jack was absent, she and Pat sat together and giggled over the same jokes and exchanged reactions about the players that turned out to be in complete accord. She drove Pat home in the red convertible, which Pat had first seen only a few weeks before when Jack identified it as Nan's car, and occasionally Pat went home with Nan to dinner.

The Camerons lived in a six-room apartment in Allandale's newest and most luxurious building overlooking the lake. They had a full-time maid, who stayed through dinner and wore a gray-nylon uniform with a white apron. All the upholstered furniture and cushions were silk damask stuffed with down, unbelievably comfortable; the rugs were fine, silky Orientals. In spite of Nan's compliments about Pat's home, Pat felt her house looked shabby compared to this. The Camerons had spent six weeks in Europe during the spring, and Nan told Pat they were all going to Mexico for Christmas.

"I'd rather travel than anything in the world," Nan said. "We're going abroad for a year when I finish high school. Mother thinks it will give me more of an idea about what I want to do in college."

"I'd like to travel," Pat said, feeling at this moment that

31

it was terribly desirable. "But I don't know when I can fit it in. Maybe when I'm married —"

Everything Nan had or wanted became important to Pat. When Pat shopped with Nan for a dress one afternoon, she was astounded at the price that Nan thought reasonable, and immediately knew that the dress had unusual distinction. Her own allowance seemed more inadequate this year than last. The sense of quality she was developing very rapidly in Nan's company was a mixed blessing.

"I love your car," she told Nan one day, as they rode home together.

"Isn't it a honey? I love it too. Dad gave it to me for my sixteenth birthday last November. I got the car when I got my license."

This seemed so reasonable that when Pat got home she brought the conversation around to having a car of her own, feeling that it probably had not occurred to her parents that she needed one.

"Well, I'm certainly glad to know that your friends have cars," her father observed with what she felt was heavy irony. "That means you won't need one, obviously."

Pat, irritated, refrained from further argument. It was apparent that he wasn't interested in her having the same advantages that her friends had. When Pat was home with her family, Nan's scale of living seemed remote and unusual. But when she was with Nan, it seemed the normal way to live.

It wasn't that Nan seemed to notice that the Marlowes lived in less luxury than the Camerons had. Indeed, she had said, more than once: "Don't you feel kind of important to have a writer for a mother? I mean, someone who gets stories in the *Post* and the *Journal* all the time?"

Mrs. Marlowe had been a professional writer for years,

and her family had become too much accustomed to the idea to think about it. But Pat loved the prestige of having new friends like Nan express such awe at knowing a writer. It made up, in some degree, for not having the same kind of clothes Nan wore.

She talked to Nan about Tim, but she had not told her they planned to get married. Some instinct warned her that Nan would not take the idea seriously, and she protected her own conviction from any incredulity as much as possible.

Frequently she talked to Nan about Jack Willis, feeling that if she could mend things between them, both would be grateful.

"Oh, I like Jack all right," Nan said carelessly. "But he was too possessive and bossy. He wanted to be serious too soon. I'm not going to settle down to one man until I've done everything I want to do first — see the world, meet dozens of men, have fun!"

"But he seemed to think you wouldn't even go out with him any more."

"I don't know about that," said Nan with great indifference. "He could be fun, but not if he keeps on feeling the way he did the last time. I tried it once, and he spent the whole evening talking about how he felt and what he wanted, and how he knew he'd made a mistake, and so on. It got so boring, I just wondered why go on?"

"I can see what you mean," Pat said, not being sure that she did. "But of course it's entirely different with Tim and me. Jack can give me advice when I need it, but we're only good friends. And I can talk to him about Tim."

"I'm dying to meet Tim," Nan said. "I don't remember him from last year at all."

"You'll meet him," Pat promised. "I don't expect him

33

home before Thanksgiving. But he's terribly homesick." She paused, remembering that his last letters had not sounded homesick at all. "At least he was," she amended, "but I think he's getting adjusted now and finding friends."

"That's good," Nan said. "Oh, I just remembered something: I'm having a birthday party on November ninth — four couples for dinner and a show downtown. Can you come? I've got a boy for you from Wilcox High."

"I'd love it," Pat accepted. "Thanks so much. It will be wonderful."

Her greatest satisfaction this year was the knowledge that she was now part of Nan's crowd, who not only wore such beautiful clothes, but did such fascinating things. Without ever spending much thought on the subject, she knew that Nan's crowd and Tim were two widely separated affections, and when she did consider the idea she dreamed of bringing them together. They would adore Tim, and he would like them, and they could all be part of a big, congenial group, perhaps for the rest of their lives. The fact that Connie was not part of her group of new friends bothered Pat, and she tried not to notice.

Connie called, in a state of excitement the next night, to tell Pat that Mike had phoned her from Princeton.

"I was so thrilled I could hardly hold the telephone," she reported. "Imagine! A long-distance call like that and so unexpected! It was lucky I was home. Anyway, he told me to call you and tell you and your folks that he is all right and having a fine time, and that he got good grades on some tests last week."

"That's good news," said Pat. "I'll tell the folks. How did he happen to call?"

"Oh, he said he wanted to talk to me." Connie sounded pleased. "I've been writing regularly, but he said he just felt like talking."

"I wish Tim would get that idea," said Pat.

It seemed so obvious, now that Mike had called, that she wondered why Tim had never thought of it, and she said so when she told her parents of Connie's message.

"Long-distance calls run into a lot of money," her mother remarked, "and I imagine Tim doesn't feel he can afford it. After all, he's writing every day."

"If only he'd call once," Pat mourned. "I'd like to hear his voice again. It would mean so much."

In her letter that night, she asked him to call her sometime, and when Tim answered he explained that college was costing more than he had expected and he seemed to be running out of money all the time. There was no answer to that problem. But Pat recalled the girl he had mentioned spending time with and found herself wondering how much money he spent on Gwen's coffee, how much on movie dates, and whether he really wanted to telephone.

It was impossible to study. Every time she sat down to concentrate on English or French or history, she would find that her eyes refused to focus on the print, that when she drove herself to read carefully her mind did not take it in, and when she was in class she could not follow what the teacher was saying for five minutes together. Her mood went up and down from day to day. When she was normally cheerful she told herself that there was no question about the disadvantages of being in love with someone who must be separated from her; when she was moody, as she found herself more and more often, she felt with deep pessimism that her love was threatened from all sides

35

and she was going to lose Tim. The more she worried the less important her studies became, because, if she lost Tim, what was the use of anything at all?

She tried to avoid being alone, for when she was alone she thought about Tim, and her thoughts were always foreboding. When she was with Nan or Connie or at the Y Club, she was momentarily distracted from her worries, and it became more and more important to keep busy, keep active, be with people all the time.

The play helped a great deal, for rehearsals took every afternoon until five o'clock, and with a little forethought she could plan to study with one of the girls almost every night. She felt as if she were racing against time. Before enough time had gone by for her marks to be really low, she must pull herself together, she must see Tim again, she must settle her state of mind. And to that end she talked to Jack Willis endlessly, she talked to Nan, she talked to Connie.

"It's one of those things you have to live through," Connie told her, with sympathy that seemed purely courtesy. "Look at my sister, Joanne: she's coming home next month to wait until Jerry gets back from sea duty. Everyone has to get along by herself some time or other, either when your man goes to college, or when he goes into service."

"Is Joanne coming home?" Pat was diverted from herself. "Oh, I'll be so glad to see her. There're so many things I'd like to talk over with her."

"She's going to have a baby next spring," Connie revealed.

"A baby!" breathed Pat. "Oh, Connie, how wonderful! You'll be an aunt! Aren't you lucky that she's going to be home?"

36

"It's pretty exciting," Connie agreed, not visibly excited. "But next spring looks like a long time away. Probably April, she thought."

"Didn't Joanne get married before she was through college?"

Connie nodded. "She married at the end of her sophomore year, when Jerry was graduating. He was going into service right away, and she wanted to go with him. She's still going to college whenever she gets a chance."

Pat's eyes were dreaming. "It sounds divine. That's what I want to ask her about."

"It sounds like a nuisance to me," Connie said flatly. "I'd rather not go back to college after I'm married. I'd like to be through with it by that time."

"But you don't know —" Pat checked herself. She had told Connie so many times that Connie didn't know what it was like to be in love that she felt repetitious and she knew that Connie would tell her that she had heard it all before. But Joanne would not have heard it.

Pat remembered Joanne well from a year and a half ago when she had married Jerry and left Allandale. A pretty, brown-haired girl with dark brows and hazel eyes, she had gone to Northwestern University in the neighboring suburb of Evanston. She had lived on campus for two years. The Reids had resisted the idea of her getting married before she was through school, Pat seemed to remember, although the arguments had meant little to her at the time. All she knew now was that she had been invited to the June wedding, that Joanne had been a beautiful bride, and then she had disappeared with her husband to some distant naval base, whence they had visited Allandale only twice since her marriage, and Pat had not seen her then.

And now she was coming home without Jerry, to wait in solitude how many months? Six, anyway. Perhaps Joanne was more unlucky than she herself was, Pat thought, just sitting at home like that with nothing to do. The thought cheered her up in some perverse fashion. Joanne would probably be moping and unhappy, even as Pat had been these past weeks, and Pat would know how to sympathize.

"How soon is she coming?" she asked Connie.

"Early November."

Something to look forward to helped to make the days go faster. It was already the nineteenth of October, and *Good Housekeeping* was being presented the next weekend. Following the performance there would be a cast party to celebrate the triumphant production, and Jack had invited Pat to go with him. Joanne would be arriving the next weekend, and then there was Nan's party, and after that Tim would be home in less than two weeks.

Pat began to feel as if life were taking shape again, and she was cheered in spite of herself.

5

The dress rehearsal for *Good Housekeeping* on Thursday ran from three in the afternoon until eight in the evening without a break, and the cast dispersed exhausted by a nerve-racking, fine-drawn effort. Jack took Pat home and said as he left, " Pull yourself together, kid; we need you tomorrow."

"I'll be right in there," Pat said, feeling that her smile was wan. "What I'm really looking forward to is Saturday." She stopped as she opened the door and turned back for a moment. "You know, these plays are strenuous! I'm beat. But by Saturday we'll be ready to celebrate — no more struggle."

He grinned from the top of the steps. "And how we'll celebrate! Don't let me down."

She went in and closed the door, feeling worn out and wondering why anyone voluntarily put herself through the grueling routine of memorizing, rehearsing, and frantic effort that she had just ended. In spite of the work, it was fun, she seemed to remember, although at this minute she was too tired to believe it.

I'll probably be right there in the front line when the

tryouts are listed for the next play, she thought with a wry smile because she felt as if the theater had taken hold of her.

She tore open Tim's letter, anticipating without pleasure that he would tell her about his last date with Gwen.

" Pat, darling,

" I'm coming home this weekend and I can hardly wait. One of the boys here, name of Maxwell, is driving to Chicago this weekend for his cousin's wedding, and I can ride along, round trip for three bucks. He's taking three of us, leaving around five in the morning, and he thinks we'll make Allandale by two o'clock. So look for me then. I'll stop off to see the folks, pick up my car, and come over to your house. So long, now. I'm studying like crazy so there won't be any assignments left for the weekend. All my love, always. Tim."

She read the letter over three times, at first dazed with delight at the thought of seeing Tim this unexpectedly, then distressed that she was going to be busy, then with a faint annoyance that he was coming into conflict with a life that was now running smoothly. She forgot the fatigue that had surrounded her after rehearsal and began thinking of all the things she must do to clear the weekend for Tim. She would have to tell Jack that she couldn't go to the cast party with him after all.

" Pat? " Her mother came in from the kitchen. " You must be starved, honey. I've got your supper in the oven. How was the rehearsal? "

" Oh, it was fine." She felt as if the rehearsal had happened a long time ago. " Did you see Tim's letter? " She waved it and read it aloud. " He's coming home! It seems

40

like forever since he went away. And I'd promised to go to the cast party with Jack Willis. What a mess! "

" You can always tell Tim you're sorry but you had made all sorts of other plans before you knew he was coming," Mrs. Marlowe said half teasingly, as if she knew the suggestion was ridiculous.

" Oh, Mother, of course I can't," Pat said immediately. " I'll have to tell Jack that Tim's coming home. He knows how things are with us. He won't mind."

" But this was the year you were going to — " her mother began, and Pat broke in: " I know, Mother. We're trying it out. Tim is going with some hag named Gwen, and I've been going out with Jack Willis. But if he can come home, naturally we want to be together. What else would you expect? "

" Nothing, of course. He can go to the play with us, if you can get a ticket for him."

" That would be fine. I'd like him to see the show. I think he'd enjoy it."

The problem seemed solved. Jack was very understanding about the cast party when Pat explained the situation to him at the Friday performance.

" Sure, I know how it is," he said when they talked it over on Friday night between scenes in the wings. " It would have been fun. But naturally Tim will want to see you. Look — why don't you bring him to the cast party, and we can all go together? "

" Why don't I? " she agreed. But privately she wondered how that would work out. If there was another girl so it would be a double date —

" Why don't you ask Connie to go with you? " she suggested. " Why don't we make it a double date? "

41

It would be fun to be double-dating with Connie again. There were times these days when Connie irritated Pat. She seemed so flighty, so irresponsible, so indifferent to the feelings of someone like Mike who cared about her. It infuriated Pat to hear Connie talking about all the boys she was going out with. And that annoyance extended to her conversation in general. It seemed suddenly as if Connie talked about nothing but the way her hair looked, the way she felt, the new dresses she was buying, how dismally tired she was today.

But it had been ages since she and Connie had double-dated, and with Tim coming in tomorrow Pat remembered how lovely it had all been last spring when she and Tim had gone out with Connie and Mike. It would be like old times again, even though it would be with Jack instead of Mike.

"Try to get Connie," she urged again. "She can be loads of fun."

"I might do that," he said, eying Connie reflectively as she left the wings and went on stage for her lines. "She's kind of cute."

The more Pat thought about it, the more it seemed like a good idea to take Tim to the party. She would like him to know her new friends, and although Tim didn't like big parties, still he might come to like them if he were exposed often enough. And he might even have changed in that respect since he had been away at college. In any case, if he didn't go, Pat couldn't go, and she'd been counting on this party ever since she began work on the play.

Thinking of the possibility of change reminded her that she had not seen him for so long that he might be entirely different now. She began to wonder if she remembered ex-

42

actly what he had been like anyway. Some of the girls had told her how college changed a boy. What if she didn't even love him any more? It was a horrifying thought, and she could hardly go to sleep Friday night for thinking about the uncertainties of tomorrow.

When the telephone rang shortly after one o'clock and Pat picked it up, she heard, "Hel-lo—" in the same drawled inflection she remembered. It was as if he had never been away.

"Why, Tim, you're here!" she cried. "Oh, I'm so glad you're early! How soon can you come over?"

"I'll be there in fifteen minutes," he said. "I just got in the house this minute and all I need to do is make sure Hortense is still running."

She raced upstairs and changed her clothes, humming gaily.

"Mom?" she called. "Tim's home! Isn't that wonderful?"

As she combed her hair and retouched her lipstick it seemed at once incredible and perfectly natural that in a few minutes she would be with Tim again. She heard Hortense stop in front of the house with a familiar rattle, and ran down to open the door.

"Tim!" she cried. "Oh, darling, I'm so glad to see you!" She threw herself into his arms.

When he released her, she stepped back to look at him.

"What have you done to your hair?" she cried. "Tim! How could you? Mother! Mother, come and see what Tim's done. He's got a crew cut. Oh, I think it looks terrible."

Smiling self-consciously, Tim ran his hand across his brush cut.

"Don't you like it? Oh, well, it'll grow. I figured as long as I was at Crandall and all the fellows have short hair I'd have it cut this way. It's a lot easier to take care of, and who cares what it looks like?"

"If you don't grow it out before summer, I'm going to get a boy cut myself."

He looked alarmed. "Don't you dare! You know how I hate short cuts on you."

"Well — I feel the same way."

She seized his hand and dragged him into the living room.

"Now sit down and tell me all about college. I could think of lots of things you didn't put in your letters." Staring thoughtfully at his hair, she added, "I guess I'll get used to it."

Mrs. Marlowe came into the living room, and Tim stood up.

"So nice to see you again, Tim. All your fans are waiting for you."

"Oh, Denny could hardly sleep last night when he heard you were coming today," Pat told him. "He'll be around any minute. You're his hero."

Tim laughed, pleased. "I'll be glad to see Denny again," he said. "Say, it's wonderful to be home."

The back door slammed.

"There's Denny now," said Pat, half fearful, half anxious to hear Denny's excitement. She looked at Tim again, and her heart turned over. He looked better than she had remembered; his face was leaner and browner, and his smile more charming. There was an air of careless strength about him, a casual confidence that seemed new and strikingly attractive. His haircut she was beginning to like: the

44

strangeness had worn off, and it did something for him, made him look more mature or something. She could not define the appeal, but it didn't matter. He was home again; he was hers; he was changed only for the better. He met her eyes and smiled as he reached out and patted her hand.

Denny came in with a springy step, tossing a football from hand to hand.

"Hiya, Tim," he said carelessly. "How long are you going to be around?"

"Hi, Denny. I'll be here until Sunday night, I guess."

"Swell. Then you can play football with me. Let's go out and have a game right now."

"Oh, come now," Tim protested. "I'm worn out with that long ride from Crandall. Anyway, I'm out of practice on football. Where's your team?"

"All the guys are coming out for practice at three o'clock. You can coach us. What did you come home for anyway?"

"Lots of things besides football," Pat said decisively. "Me, for instance."

Denny looked incredulous. "Ya mean he came all the way home from college to see you?"

They all laughed uproariously, and Denny looked sulky.

"Why not?" Tim asked. "Girls are worth quite a lot of trouble, Denny. You'll find out someday."

"There's a new girl in my room this year," Denny remarked. "She's quite a dish. She wanted me to go to the movies with her today."

"*She* asked *you?*" Pat demanded.

"Sounds forward to me," said Tim, grinning. "Watch out for forward women, Denny. They'll marry you before you know it."

Pat pounded him, and he held up his arms in defense, laughing helplessly.

"Well, so long," said Denny, looking disgusted. "I'm going out and meet the team. Will you coach us sometime?"

"Not this weekend," Tim declined. "Maybe some other time when Pat's busy. But today I've got to take her out for a walk or she won't speak to me again."

"You bet I won't," Pat agreed. "It's a gorgeous day, and we're going to walk along the lake, Mother."

She picked up a short coat, and they went out to look at Tim's 1940 Ford together.

"'My sweet Hortense, she ain't good-looking, but she's got good sense,'" Pat murmured. "I missed Hortense this fall."

"So did I," said Tim, as they turned away to walk toward the lake. "I missed the car almost as much as I missed you."

"I'll bet you've been missing me," she gibed. "All those dates you were having with Gwen."

"Oh, Gwen kept me company so I wouldn't be lonesome," Tim assured her. "She's a nice kid, but I couldn't get interested in her."

"I should hope not! Can't I rely on you to be faithful for even a couple of months?"

"Now don't start complaining too soon," Tim cautioned. "After all, you haven't been sitting around by yourself either while I've been gone."

"Oh, well, I've been just passing the time," Pat said. "You'll meet all the kids tonight. I'd better tell you about tonight. First there's the play."

"Is that tonight?" He sounded dismayed, as if he'd

never heard about the play before.

"I told you about it," she reminded him. "Maybe I haven't mentioned lately that tonight is the last performance. But I thought you'd like to see it anyway, and I got a ticket for you to sit with the folks tonight."

He nodded. "At least I can keep an eye on you."

"Then afterward we're going to the cast party."

"No, ma'am," said Tim promptly. "You know how I feel about big parties — especially where I don't know anybody."

"You'll know all these kids — they were around last year. Now, Tim, listen to me. This is a very special thing. I've wanted to go to a cast party ever since I first heard about them, and this is the first time I've ever had a chance. I was going to go with Jack Willis, but when I heard you were coming home, naturally I told him I couldn't."

"Naturally."

"But we talked it over, and he thought it would be fun if we all went together. He's taking Connie, so it'll be a double date. And it won't cost you anything."

"Well, that's a consideration. O.K., then. I thought we could go off somewhere by ourselves the first time I've been home this fall. But if this is the way it's got to be, this is the way it'll be."

"That's my sweetheart," she soothed him tenderly. "You'll have fun, Tim, you really will. I think you'll enjoy big parties when you get used to them."

He looked down at her with an expression of not believing a word she said but humoring her as a fanciful woman.

"Isn't this a beautiful day?" Pat demanded, feeling that all problems had been settled. "Oh, Tim, I'm so glad

47

you're home! Look at that yellow birch over there, over-hanging the water. I love fall."

He squeezed her arm and let out a deep sigh of content-ment.

"This is what I've been waiting for ever since I got to Crandall. Maybe I can manage to get home more often now that I'm acquainted with some of the boys who drive in to Chicago once in a while."

"Tell me about Gwen," Pat said, settling herself on a rock overlooking the water. "How did you happen to meet her?"

"Oh, she's a little blond doll," he said. "She's in my English class and she kind of made up to me the first week. I'm lucky, I guess. With five boys to a girl down there, most of the freshmen don't date at all."

"Why, you lucky boy!" Pat said scathingly. "So she pursued you! And how often do you see her? Once a week? Twice a week?"

He glanced at her uneasily, aware that she was not as pleased over his good fortune as her words might indicate.

"Not too often," he said cautiously. "Of course, she's in this English class, and we go out and have a cup of coffee once in a while. Then on Friday nights we usually go to a movie. And there's some college thing going on al-most every Saturday."

"So you see her every single day for some kind of date!" Pat was suddenly, violently angry. "We're supposed to get married someday, and that ought to mean some kind of going steady — at least a little — "

"Not this year, we aren't," he reminded her. "We were supposed to go out with other people, and what about this Jack Willis you've been writing about? Every single letter you've been seeing Jack, and he's so funny, the big clown, you're having a wonderful time."

"But Jack doesn't mean a thing to me," she cried. "He's still crazy about Nan. He's in the play with me, and we've gone to a couple of school dances, and that's about all. He's only filling in an empty place while you're gone."

"But that's all Gwen is doing for me. It's different when you're living on campus. You seem to see the same people every time you turn around. It's nothing like a date every time."

"Except that you have to pay for her coffee and her movie and it costs you money out of your pocket when you're too poor to telephone home," she flashed.

He laughed aloud and patted her hand.

"Now, honey, you're being jealous, and it's flattering, but it's ridiculous. Do you want me to sit around all year and talk to no one except a couple of sad sacks that can't get girls?"

"But I should think you'd like to spend more time with the boys," she argued. "Aren't the boys any fun at all?"

"Sure they're fun. And after ten o'clock when we're in the dorm we horse around like anything. But I happen to like girls too."

"How can you tell you aren't going to like her too much?" Pat was sulky with fear and tried not to show it.

"I can tell right now," he said. "The only reason I write you about Gwen is because I want you to know everything I'm doing, everyone I'm going out with. You and I are already a team. You've got nothing to worry about till that breaks down."

"I'd feel better if you didn't take her to movies," Pat brooded. "Dances, O.K. You need a girl to dance with. But why can't you just go to the movies with the boys? "

"I probably will from now on," he said. "I'll keep this business of Gwen even more casual. O.K.? "

"Fine," she said, feeling as if she had fought a battle and won a major victory. "And you'll meet all my friends tonight. You'll love the party," she promised him.

6

The cast was assembled in the wings, the director was making his last suggestions, the actors were recalling each other's achievements in last night's performance, and the prompter looked through the curtains to report that half the audience was still coming in, although it was curtain time. Pat felt a nervous compulsion to start biting her nails and she resolutely folded her arms, holding her hands firmly under her elbows as all eyes watched the clock.

At eight twenty-seven the audience was seated and expectant, the curtain rose, and the play began.

Pat was sure the entire cast was playing its peak performance. She knew that she herself had never done so well. She managed to keep her eyes off the audience, as she had promised herself she must, and discovered, safely back in the wings, that she could not have seen Tim had she tried.

The curtain went down upon resounding applause, the cast took six curtain calls, which were two more than on Friday night, and the play was over.

Backstage the parents and friends of the actors swarmed around to exclaim over and over: " You were simply wonderful, all of you. Everyone was outstanding. I never saw such a polished performance. You were all wonderful." Each actor, each member of the production staff received his meed of acclaim.

"Why didn't Tim come back with you?" Pat asked her mother, who was telling Nan what a fine job she had done with the lead.

"He said he'd see you off stage," Mrs. Marlowe said. "You know how men are — they never like to go back-stage. Your father and he stayed together. Tim said for you to hurry up."

"Tell him I'll be out in five minutes," Pat said. "I'll take off the make-up right now and change."

There was the usual delay in changing. She had to stoop and peer over the shoulders of three other actors to see the mirror, the box of cleansing tissues was empty, and no one knew where there was more. Pat finally discovered a roll of paper towels, but towels were scratchy and slower than tissues would have been. She combed her hair and could not find the belt for her skirt nor her purse.

When she finally emerged fifteen minutes later, Tim was alone and growing impatient.

"Always the last one out," he said. "How come it takes you so much longer than anyone else? Connie was through five minutes ago. She said she and Jack would go on and meet us at the party."

"I couldn't find my purse," Pat said, annoyed at his criticism. "It had gotten under some of the costumes, and I hunted for hours before I found it. Where are the folks?"

"They went on. They said that since they'd already told you how good the play was they thought they wouldn't wait."

"I hope they know this party goes on till two thirty,"

Pat brooded. "I told them all the details, but I was going to tell them again."

"There's no rule about staying to the bitter end," said Tim.

"Now, Tim, if you spoil this party for me, I'll never speak to you again," Pat declared. "You'll have to learn to have a good time with me or I'm not going out with you."

"Honey, I always have a good time with you," he soothed her. "Don't be looking for trouble. I was only remarking that you don't have to stay to the end if you don't want to."

"All right," Pat said agreeably. "If we're both having a good time, the sky's the limit."

He grinned at her, and she melted into happy confidence. Of course he would have a good time.

At Tony's house the party was well under way when they arrived. Connie and Jack were watching for them. The house was swarming with high school students: cast members, dates, production staff, members of the make-up committee, the ticket committee; everyone who had had any part in the play was there.

"Hi, Connie," said Tim. He shook hands with Jack, smiled at everyone he met, and entered into the spirit of the evening beautifully. Pat felt with pride that he was a wonderful man to be with and that he was having just as good a time as she had promised him he would. It was only eleven thirty.

The food was being set out on the table: the cakes contributed by the girls, the doughnuts and potato chips brought by the boys, the Cokes and soft drinks supplied by the hospitality committee. With food in hand, the boys and girls converged around the piano where one of the boys was beating out some rhythmic jazz.

Tim took Pat's plate back in the dining room, and then they danced. The room became crowded and then hot as the dancers circled in tiny areas of the floor.

"I could use another drink," said Tim after a few minutes. "How many kids are here, do you suppose?"

"About sixty," Pat said, glancing around. "Look, Dave is going to play songs from last spring's music festival."

As he played, the dancers left the floor and crowded around the piano again, singing the music they remembered. They sang for an hour and then couples began to drift away and look for something else to do. Dave was through playing the piano, he announced with loud, final chords. Jack was examining the record collections that some of the boys had brought with them.

"Here's something good," he said. "Let's hear this."

He put his selection on the record player and turned up the volume so that everyone could hear the music from the newest musical show. Then, as if he were unaware of anyone around, he began to pantomime his appreciation of the music, raising his hands and putting on an expression of horror at a soprano, covering his ears and cowering from a high note, beating time like a comical conductor, applauding primly like an overstuffed dowager with a lorgnette. The crowd watched him, knowing what to expect and convulsed with laughter. Pat thought it was the funniest thing she had ever seen. Even Tim was laughing, albeit reluctantly.

It was going on one o'clock, and the teachers who had been enjoying the party as much as any of the students began to make their farewells, talking to Dave about his piano playing, to Tony about what a nice party it was, to the cast members, to Tony's parents.

Jack seemed unaware that anyone was leaving or that anyone was watching him. With studious attention to the record, he went on and on with his pantomime.

"That guy never knows when to stop," Tim murmured to Pat. "After a while it isn't funny any more."

Pat felt defensive about Jack, whom she considered funny no matter how long he clowned, and yet protective about Tim's enjoyment for which she felt responsible. She wished Jack would stop, and she hated to leave until he did, sensing his awareness of an audience, regardless of his apparent lack of attention.

With the departure of the teachers, the party was beginning to loosen up a little. Jack's audience drifted away, groups sat quietly talking in different corners, and Connie was out in the dining room filling another plate. Nan was sitting in a dark corner talking seriously with Dick Burton, with whom she was going fairly steadily. When Pat saw them, Dick met her eyes with a somber, judicial stare that left her uncomfortable.

"What do we do now?" Tim wanted to know as the record ended and Jack turned around with a vacant stare and then dived for the dining room with the expression of a starving castaway in sight of land. A burst of laughter followed him, and he turned and took a low bow of appreciation.

"We could eat some more," Pat suggested.

Tim grimaced. "I've had enough to eat. How about leaving pretty soon?"

"Leaving!" she was outraged. "Why, it's only one thirty. This party will go on for ages yet."

"That's what I'm afraid of. We've had it, haven't we? What else are we going to do? Watch that clown for the rest of the night?"

"Don't you *like* Jack?" Pat asked, unable to believe the implications of Tim's question.

"Nope." Tim selected some pretzel sticks and ate them slowly. "He's all right for a while. But pretty soon you feel as if you've seen the picture about six times and that's often enough."

Pat picked up another bottle of iced Coke. "I thought you were having a good time, Tim. What's the trouble? Don't you like to have fun?"

"Sure I do," he maintained. "And I did tonight. Trouble is, now I've had enough. It isn't fun forever. I'm ready to go home. We've been here a couple of hours, and everything is beginning to repeat itself."

Pat sucked thoughtfully on her iced drink, feeling that this was some kind of crisis. She hated the thought of missing any of the fun. She hated to leave, to give up before she had to. As long as anything was going on, it was worth seeing, even if they had seen it six times.

Uncertain whether to insist on staying, she moved away from the dining room back into the other rooms, seeking an excuse. Some of the lights had been turned off. The party was quieting down too much.

Suddenly Pat decided to leave. Tim was highly critical of couples who wanted to display their affection in public, and it was important to salvage as much as possible of the pleasure of the party that had started on such a hilarious note.

"All right, let's go," she said to Tim. "It's beginning to break up anyway."

"I'm worn out. I'm ready to get some sleep and start

56

over tomorrow," Tim muttered.

"I might have known you wouldn't enjoy it," she said in the car, sulky now and no longer resisting her mood.

"Well, what was there in it for me?" he demanded, responding to her irritation. "The food was good, and the dancing was pretty good while it lasted — for about twenty minutes. But I can't see any great entertainment in edging around between people to cross the room, and standing up all night because there's such a crowd, and the whole last half hour was Jack Willis, and I was tired of him before we went to the party."

Pat turned sharply toward him and drew in her breath with a suddenness that made her cough.

"Why, I thought Jack was wonderful," she said positively. "I certainly can't understand you. Everyone else was having hysterics."

"Maybe that was the trouble," he said grimly. "I don't seem to have hysterics as easily as everyone else."

They pulled up for a red light, and he turned toward her appeasingly and reached for her hand. "Don't be mad, honey. I've always been like this, and you knew it right from the beginning. I might have thought Jack was a lot funnier if I liked him better, but I don't like him and I'll probably never like anything he does."

The touch of his hand broke her angry mood, and she squeezed it encouragingly, realizing that there was more behind this wrangle than she had thought.

"Why don't you like Jack?" she asked. "Really, honey, I want to know because I've had so much fun with him this year that I thought you'd like him too."

He released his hand to set the car in motion as the light changed.

"That's probably the reason, if I want to be frank about

57

it," he muttered. "It drives me nuts to think of you having so much fun with somebody else."

She laughed at him affectionately, her good disposition quite restored.

"You old party pooper," she jeered. "You did pretty well after all, I guess. And if you don't want to laugh at Jack Willis, you don't have to. But don't forget I feel exactly the same way about Gwen, the hussy!"

He smiled, answering her teasing noncommittally, and, reassured, she began to chatter about plans for Sunday.

"Tomorrow is supposed to be another lovely day," she said, "and Connie thought it would be fun to have a picnic out in the woods. I told her it was a sensational idea. We'll go about twelve o'clock while the sun is high."

He glanced at her, and his face was set in an expression of sad resignation. They pulled up in front of her house, and he stopped the motor and turned toward her.

"You go ahead," he said. "You love picnics, and I can't stand them, but I wouldn't want to spoil your fun. I think I'll take the bus back to Crandall anyway, about ten tomorrow morning."

She stared at him wide-eyed. "Why, Tim, you can't go so soon," she wailed. "You only got in this afternoon. I was counting on your being here tomorrow. What made you decide to leave so early?"

He patted her hand again. "You're so busy and you have so many plans and everything. What's the use of my sticking around? I thought we could be alone together for at least one date on the weekend and talk things over and everything. If we're always going to be in a mob of people, I'd rather not stay."

He stared out of the windshield as if he were preparing

58

himself for sacrifice, and she thought rapidly and deeply, realizing that if he left she would be alone again, in spite of plans and friends.

"Look, honey," she pleaded, holding his hand while she talked. "I really thought you'd like to go out in the woods. But if you wouldn't, I wouldn't either. I'd rather be with you than anything. And when you're not happy, neither am I. I'll tell Connie we're not dating with them at all. Now what did you want to do tomorrow?"

He brightened at once. Boys are boys, she thought, whether they are big or small.

"I'd kind of like to go to church with you at eleven," he said, "the way we did last year. And then I'd like you to have dinner with me at my folks' house. In the afternoon I thought we could take Hortense out and ride along the lake and talk. Maxwell will pick me up about six."

"I think that would be a wonderful day," Pat said. "It's a much better idea than the picnic, Tim."

"You're sure you don't mind giving up the picnic?" he demanded anxiously.

She nodded slowly, even as she was thinking of the fallen leaves, the snapping fire, the songs with Jack's guitar, the lonely, lovely magic of the forest in the fall.

She would have loved the day outdoors, she acknowledged to herself. But if Tim did not enjoy it, her own enjoyment would be spoiled, and there was nothing either one of them could do about it, because that was how it was. She would rather be with him; she would rather see him happy than follow her own preference.

When he had left her, she went slowly upstairs still thinking about the choice she was making, whether she was right or wrong, and what kind of life they would have together. Last spring her mother had talked about their common interests, which were few, and Pat had told her blithely that they would build them together.

Now she wondered how that would work out. And yet it had to, she told herself fiercely, because without Tim there would be nothing at all.

7

She dressed carefully for church the next morning, glad that Tim had suggested it.

The sermon was about trying to share the other person's point of view and seemed singularly appropriate. Pat felt, as they drove back to Tim's house for dinner with his parents, that he had made a great effort last night to understand her passion for crowds of people, and she was prepared to make as great an effort on her own part to understand his preference for other kinds of entertainment.

Mrs. Davis was delighted to have her with them. Tim opened up when Pat was there and talked about college experiences that his mother told Pat he never seemed to discuss when they were alone. Pat felt that she was almost a part of the family, but there was still a sense of constraint, of having to be on her good behavior, of being careful to make a good impression. She could not relax with the Davises as she could with her own parents, who knew exactly how bad she could be when she tried and seemed not to hold it against her. It was important to make Mrs. Davis think that she was a nice girl to take into the family.

That reminded her of the stories she had read about

young couples who moved in with one of the families, and the thought turned her cold. She would not want to continue living with her own family after she was married, nor did she want to be with the Davises, who had plenty of room to take in a young couple. She wondered if that alternative would keep her from getting married.

But it was a question that did not come up when she and Tim were out together in the afternoon. They found a dozen other things to talk about besides marriage: Tim's straight A record in his math courses, the trouble he was having with freshman English, what ambitions Pat had besides getting married.

"You ought to be thinking about your college right now," he advised her. "You know how hard it is to get into college these days."

"I might go to Crandall," she said comfortably.

They thought about the fun of being together in college, and then Tim became serious again.

"I'd like to have you there," he said, "but it's not a very good reason for choosing your college. What are you going to study for? What do you want to do later on?"

She laughed. "I want to get married. What else?"

He laughed too, and hugged her close.

"But seriously," he said, "I've learned a lot since freshman year began. College is too expensive to fool around with. You ought to have a goal so you can get as much out of it as possible. You ought to have a good reason for choosing any college."

Pat made light of the idea.

"Goals!" she repeated. "Remember when Mrs. Stevens talked to the high school assembly a year ago? I remember as clearly as if it were yesterday, because she was so good.

She talked about having a goal, and I thought about it every once in a while, and then I met you, and after that any other goal got kind of hazy."

Tim hugged her again but he was not to be diverted. "There has to be some reason why you want to go to college," he insisted. "I'm beginning to have a lot of respect for education. That's one thing college has done for me so far. I wouldn't want a wife who didn't go if she could, but I wouldn't want you to go without any purpose at all."

Pat sobered down. "I know. But I haven't found out yet what I want to do. Last year I thought I'd like to teach. Someday I'll know, I suppose. Maybe I'll want to go into theater work. It was a lot of fun working in that play, and I could see things I wanted to learn more about."

"But if you decide on a school of speech, Crandall isn't good for that."

She was tired of this serious discussion.

"I'll find something," she said, with a note of closing the subject. "I'll give the whole thing a lot of thought and decide on something before you come home for Christmas."

They sat and looked at the lake in the late autumn light, with the crisp northeast wind fresh against their faces. The waves were rolling in, gray and rhythmic, foaming on the shore or breaking in high-dashing spray against the bulkhead. A white drift of gulls rode the gray water far out, and one lone sailboat heeled before the wind.

"Isn't this lovely?" said Pat, with an overwhelming sense of happiness. It was almost too perfect to be alone with Tim and the lake and the rushing wind.

"I'm glad we spent the day this way," she said softly. The delight of their solitude with beauty mounted

63

slowly, as they sat on the rock watching the water, and Pat felt that she had discovered a new meaning in life that she had never known before. If she had insisted on the picnic with another couple, the day would have gone by in jesting and song and hilarity. It would have been fun. But this afternoon had been so much more. She felt that she and Tim had deepened their understanding in subtle ways that were true and lasting. Even their silences were charged with satisfaction.

All too soon the afternoon was ending, the time was gone, and Tim had to get home to pack and be ready when Maxwell came to pick him up. It seemed as if he'd been home only a moment, and Pat felt as if she couldn't bear to say good-by again.

She thought, Parting is like dying a little, and she felt as if she had discovered all by herself some deep truth of life.

She didn't say it out loud, because she had a feeling that it had been said before. But it was comforting to know that someone else had discovered the same pain and put it into words that fit her own need. It would be interesting tonight, when Tim was gone, to hunt up that quotation and find out who had said it. Some intellectual curiosity began to flicker with a faint light, and by that light she could discern, although dimly, what Tim had meant when he said he wanted his wife to go to college.

She had so much to think about since he had been home. That was one of the reasons why she loved him. She admired him for many things, and one of them was his mature attitude toward preparing himself for life. She wished she could feel about it as he did, and it occurred to her that if she really worked at it, perhaps she would feel that way before she was through growing up.

It would not be too long until Tim would be home again for Thanksgiving, Pat kept telling herself as she drove home alone when he had gone. She thought ahead, trying to fill her mind with enough anticipation to overcome the melancholy that depressed her. Next week Joanne Reid would be home. Only she wasn't Joanne Reid any more. She was Joanne Miner now, Mrs. Jerry Miner, who would be staying with her mother and father waiting for her husband to come home from the Navy.

Pat felt that she and Joanne must have a lot in common: each separated from her loved one, each trying to pass the endless time, each with no purpose but to wait. She could think of all sorts of things to ask Joanne, questions no one else would be able to answer for her.

She called Connie that evening to talk over the weekend, Tim's leave-taking, Joanne's coming, her plan to see Joanne as soon as possible. It was a surprise to learn that Joanne was going back to her old job as soon as she arrived.

"But I thought she was going to have a baby!" Pat exclaimed.

"Oh, she is," Connie assured her. "But not until next April. Anyway, she wrote her office and said that if they needed a secretary for a few months, she'd take the job, and they wrote right back and said they could always use her, that they'd never been able to find another girl as good as she was. Mother is terribly pleased, because she and Joanne both thought it was going to get pretty tedious sitting around the house waiting for time to pass."

"Well, for goodness' sake," Pat uttered, dumfounded. She had assumed so certainly that Joanne would prefer never to work again if she didn't have to. This threw a whole new light on attitudes toward waiting for your heart's desire. She would have to reconsider some of the things she had planned to ask Joanne.

"Anyway, I hope I'll have a chance to see her sometime," she said. "Do you suppose she'd remember me?"

"Of course she remembers you," said Connie. "I wrote her about you and Tim long ago."

"That's good," said Pat.

She loved the idea that everyone knew that she and Tim were going to get married someday. It seemed to insure the future, the more so when adults outside the high school crowd took the news seriously. For the same reason it irritated her that Connie seemed so casual about Mike. Because she and Mike had discovered each other soon after Pat and Tim had fallen in love, Pat felt as if they ought to stay in love too.

"Have you heard from Mike lately?" she asked.

"I had a letter Friday," said Connie. "I haven't had a minute to answer it yet, but I'll get around to it. He sounds busy."

"He probably thinks you don't write often enough."

"Probably." Connie sounded indifferent. "It doesn't seem the same when he is so far away. I have no idea how things are going to be when I see him at Christmas."

"Well" — Pat was not sure how much further to inquire into Mike's affairs — "tell Joanne I'll come over and see her."

"Come any time," Connie urged. "I know she'll be delighted to see you again."

Joanne arrived on Friday as scheduled, Pat learned the next weekend from Connie, and looked wonderful —

blooming and happy and energetic and not moping at all. This seemed to Pat miraculous or else unfeeling, and she got herself invited to come over and see Joanne on Saturday afternoon.

Joanne had always been pretty, with a slimly rounded figure and a light step and buoyant gaiety. But now she was more than pretty; she was charming, with a new air of maturity that seemed to set her years away from Pat, and at the same time she was sincerely interested in Pat's affairs and quickly responsive. She was knitting a cherry-colored dress, which would be right for next spring, she said.

"I don't see how you can stand it to be separated from Jerry for so long," Pat said frankly, when they had been talking for a few minutes.

Joanne shrugged. "It happens to everyone sometime," she said. "He couldn't take me with him. A girl has to learn to stand on her own feet in this life, and if her man has to go off in another direction to do a job, she must develop some kind of strength to carry her along till he comes back again. Thank goodness, I can go back to my job for a few months. The main thing is to be doing something that needs doing, and the time will go quickly."

Pat tried to apply the words to herself. "Something that needs doing" — she suspected that when she found that elusive purpose she would have found the goal she kept hearing about. But right this minute it all seemed to apply only to somebody else, someone like Joanne who was already married. Pat rose to leave.

"I'm glad you're here while you're waiting," she told Joanne. "I never really had a chance to know you before but now I want to, and maybe you can help me with some of the questions that bother me from time to time."

" I'd love to," Joanne said cordially.

The questions that had seemed so important all last week now seemed foolish. But Pat went home with a new poise. Seeing Joanne made her realize that her own separation was not really as difficult as she had been fancying it.

8

Jack Willis called the day after Tim left and he talked for half an hour. He was talking less about Nan these days and more about Pat, and she knew the delightful assurance of being attractive to more than one boy. Of course, with Jack it meant nothing more than a flattering compliment, she thought, smiling at herself in the mirror. But it was fun. And next Friday was the long-awaited birthday party to which Nan had invited her. Her date that night would be someone from Wilcox High. It was hard to say whether she spent more time wondering what Benny would be like or thinking of the show Nan was taking them to see. The whole evening sounded as glamorous and delightful as a dream.

Her father dropped her at Nan's apartment at six, and she went up alone, looking at her hair and lipstick while she rode up in the elevator, checking her stocking seams again, and knowing confidently that in spite of its low price her taffeta cocktail dress was very flattering.

"Pat!" Nan met her at the door. "I'm so glad you're here. Come right in and meet these other people. You know Marcia and Lynn."

Marcia Pettit, tall and blond and suave, was one of

the outstanding girls in the school, and Pat had always admired her, feeling that Marcia was entirely out of her own orbit. Lynn Howard was brown-haired, brown-eyed, and aloof, outstanding in tennis and swimming, with no time for those outside her own circle. Pat considered her a snob. Now she smiled at Pat distantly.

"And this is Bill Talbot." Nan took her across the room, where Bill stood up and said, "Nice to know you," with a friendly smile. Bill had been going with Marcia since last Christmas, Pat knew. She met Warren Willson, who was going with Lynn. The boys were more friendly than the girls, she thought fleetingly. And then she met Dick Burton, whom she did not like — a quiet boy who looked at people with a brooding stare as if he were forming opinions about them. Pat always felt sure the opinions were unflattering. He was interested in science and had very high grades, and Pat felt that he looked down on students with lesser talents. Tonight he was as brooding and pensive as ever. He nodded at her indifferently and said hi with a half smile.

"Now all we're waiting for is Pat's date," said Nan. "He's coming from up the shore, so he's a little late." She turned to Pat. "Benny Frazer. He goes to Wilcox High, so you probably don't know him, but he's awfully nice. My folks have been friends of his family ever since we were born."

The doorbell chimed, and she darted to answer.

When she returned she was wearing a white orchid corsage. Pat was so fascinated with the orchid that she didn't notice the stranger until Nan brought him to her and said, "Pat, this is Benny Frazer."

"Hi," said Benny, smiling at her politely. He was a tall,

70

heavy-set youth with blond hair, colorless eyebrows, small blue eyes, and an air of bewilderment.

Oh, well, thought Pat hopefully, maybe he will turn out to be dazzling when I get to know him better. Benny moved uncertainly across the room and sat down beside Dick, who seemed to know him, and the girls went into the bedroom for their coats.

"Nan, your orchid is simply gorgeous," Marcia breathed rapturously.

"You like it?" Nan glanced down at the corsage. "I do too. Benny gave it to me. Wasn't it darling of him?"

Pat stared at it, and a shaft of longing pierced her soul. She had never worn an orchid in her life, and she felt as if nothing was quite so desirable or luxurious. She hoped passionately that someone, preferably Tim, would give her an orchid soon. Maybe for Christmas, she thought dreamily.

Pat and Benny rode with Nan and Dick in the Camerons' car. The two other couples drove down in Warren Willson's car to meet the party at the club. The division was disappointing to Pat; she had looked forward to chummy conversation with Marcia and Lynn. But she tried to make the best of this occasion to become better acquainted with Benny, although her lack of confidence about Dick was a handicap.

"You go to Wilcox High?" she inquired.

"Yes."

"What is your favorite subject?"

"Science."

"Oh, like Dick Burton. Science is so important these days. Where are you going next year?"

"Cal Tech."

"Are you going into electronics? They say electronic engineers are needed so badly."

"Nope. Chemistry."

This was very heavy going, so she took a deep breath and looked out of the window for a few minutes, thinking, If he wants to talk, let him speak up. But when he did speak it was to ask a question of Dick, who answered as briefly as Benny himself.

Pat wondered if it was the presence of the Camerons that inhibited conversation. She sat up a little so she could see Nan, riding with her parents in front, and said, "Did you say you're going to Mexico for Christmas, Nan?"

"We hope to." Mrs. Cameron turned her head slightly from the front seat. "It's still a little early to be sure."

Pat gave up any effort at conversation and looked at the brilliantly lighted shop windows the rest of the way into town. Nan talked a little, mostly about private affairs with Dick.

At the University Club they found the rest of their party, and the girls went into the ladies' cloakroom to leave their coats. Pat glanced from her own well-worn fleece coat to the coats the other girls were handing to the check girl, and then looked away again, disliking the contrast. Nan stood in front of the long mirror, pinning her orchid in place on her short-sleeved cocktail dress, and envy possessed Pat again.

Through dinner she kept looking at the orchid. It seemed terribly important for Tim to realize what it meant to her, to make the supreme gesture of divining what she wanted and to give it to her.

The party sat around a large table for ten, and Mrs. Cameron directed questions and conversation with skill.

The food was delicious and lavish. But talk languished. No one chattered spontaneously; no one told any funny stories. Everyone answered politely: " Yes, thank you, Mrs. Cameron. My steak is delicious." " This is just the way I like it, thank you." " No, thank you, Mrs. Cameron, I don't notice any draft." " Yes, I'm very comfortable, thank you." Between these considerate questions and reassuring answers, each girl, who sat next to her own date, chatted with him in subdued tones. Pat turned to Benny and tried again.

" That is a beautiful corsage you gave Nan," she said, putting forth all her sparkle and vivacity.

" It's O.K.," he said indifferently, directing a reluctant glance at the orchid. " Mom's idea."

She would have been more encouraged if it had been his own idea, and she dropped that subject.

" I'm dying to see this show tonight, aren't you? I've been hearing about it ever since it opened in New York. Doesn't it sound terrific? "

He nodded, working on a mouthful of steak, and she ate some salad. After a moment she spoke again.

" Did you see Katharine Cornell last winter in her first TV performance? She was tremendous."

" No, I didn't see her."

She received a strong impression that he had never heard of Katharine Cornell, so she tried another subject.

" Are you going with anyone at Wilcox High? I know the cutest girl there, Shirley Baker. She was at a summer place where we were a couple of years ago and she's darling."

" Don't know her."

He hadn't told her whether he went with anyone or not, but by this time Pat was convinced that no girl in her right mind would ever go out with him. He was a complete dud. With a sweet smile for Benny, to cover her revulsion, she turned toward Dick Burton on the other side of her. He was staring at Marcia across the table as if he were trying to decide whether she was worth knowing or not, and when Pat spoke he glanced toward her as if he disliked the interruption and then with a brief answer resumed his study of Marcia.

Pat gave up and concentrated on enjoying the food, since there was nothing else to enjoy. If Tim were only with her, she thought longingly! It crossed her mind that perhaps the reason she had never belonged to the "big crowd" before was because she didn't fit in. Certainly she would not want to spend very much time with these friends of Nan's whom she was meeting tonight, and yet she knew Nan was with them most of the time.

Her eye fell on the orchid corsage again, and she wondered if Nan ever found this company dull, and how much dullness you must endure to wear orchids.

Dinner was over at last, and some constraint seemed to have been loosened. Back in the cloakroom the girls talked more freely, assuring Nan that this was a wonderful evening, and including Pat with occasional glances and smiles in their conversation. She was feeling at home with them now, and the disappointment of the earlier part of the evening had disappeared. The boys didn't count, in the "big crowd." It was the girls who mattered, and these girls were friendly after all.

The musical show was as enthralling as Pat had anticipated, and even the fact that she was still sitting between Benny and Dick could not dim her pleasure; there was no need to talk. The seats were in the tenth row, and Pat had never sat so close to the stage before. She enjoyed the luxury of the show to the fullest, quite aware of the cost of the tickets, and convinced that they were worth every cent of the price.

Even during the intermission, while Benny read his program in silence for fifteen minutes, she felt at once dreamy and gay as she went out to the lobby with the rest of the party and stood in the midst of ladies in mink and gentlemen in dinner jackets.

If Tim had been with her, she thought again, the evening would have been absolutely perfect.

9

How was the birthday party? " Mrs. Marlowe inquired the next morning when Pat came down for a late breakfast.

"It was heavenly! " said Pat, forgetting every frustration. "Mother, it was gorgeous! Money does make a difference, doesn't it? "

"Quite a lot," said her mother. "I mean, in the things it will buy. The real question is how important are those things."

"Plenty important," said Pat positively. "Nan had an orchid — the most heavenly thing you ever saw. I wish Tim would give me one sometime."

"I imagine he'd like to. But orchids are expensive and he doesn't have much money. You have to keep things in proportion, you know."

"I know," Pat sighed. "Why couldn't I have fallen in love with a millionaire? It ought to be just as easy."

"Lots of girls have thought so," her mother observed, "but it's not a rule to depend on."

"Oh, well " — Pat was trying to be philosophical — " it was nice while it lasted. Maybe it will happen again sometime. I wish Tim would call me long-distance once in a while. Mike calls Connie all the time."

"I know he does." Her mother sounded disgusted. "He could almost pay his fare home by now with the tolls he's paid for telephone calls. Tim can't spend money like that, Pat. Be reasonable and don't bother him about it."

"If he didn't buy coffee for Gwen and take her out to movies, he'd have more money," Pat brooded. "If I ever get to Crandall for that dance he keeps talking about, I'll certainly show her!"

Her mother left the kitchen as if she thought the conversation was too foolish to reply to, and Pat stared at the saltcellar, which had apples painted on it to match their kitchen china. The warm, dreamy memory of luxury from last night had evaporated, leaving only discontentment. Moodily she went back to her room to change her bed and look over the clothes that seemed more and more worn and undistinguished as she looked at them.

She kept thinking that only two weeks ago Tim had been home and she wanted to see him again. If he were here, she told herself, she wouldn't feel this way about her clothes, or having no money, or *anything*. If they were married, everything would be so different. *Why* must they wait?

There was no answer to that. She tried to think of something else, wondering what Connie was doing tonight. But she knew that answer: Connie was going out with Bob McDougal and quite thrilled about it. Pat spent a few minutes hating Connie because of the way she was treating Mike, and then turned her thoughts to Nan and immediately felt better. She could call Nan up and talk to her about the party.

Bouncing off the bed where she had thrown herself, in

a mood that soared from depression to gaiety with the turn of a thought, she went to the telephone.

"Nan? Hi, this is Pat. That was a wonderful party last night. I loved every minute of it. Why, of course I liked Benny. He seemed a little hard to know, if you know what I mean — kind of quiet and everything. But he has lots of possibilities. . . . I certainly appreciated your having me and I never ate such food. What are you doing this afternoon? I thought we might go shopping if you didn't have other plans, since there is no football game today . . ."

Nan could always shop, but Pat felt that her life was sordid and confined, compared to Nan's delightful existence, when she discovered later that she had to do at least an hour's ironing before she could leave. However, she negotiated a change of time with Nan and rushed at top speed to clean her room and do the ironing.

As she ironed, the thought of getting married recurred. It seemed more logical all the time; if both parents paid the tuition, she and Tim could earn the rest. Why, by this time next year she could be keeping house for Tim!

When she put on her best suit to meet Nan at Maynard's, she had her own home practically furnished. She was sure Tim would feel about it exactly as she did when she talked to him on his next trip home.

As they left Maynard's, Pat stopped to gaze in the window of Rundall's gift shop, which had Allandale's most distinctive selection of silver, china, lamps, and wedding gifts. The window was edged with silver spoons in all patterns, and Pat looked from one to another.

If she could pick out a silver pattern, relatives could give her pieces of silver for Christmas. But Tim seemed to like almost no pattern that she liked, and so far they had not

78

been able to settle on any choice. It was typical, she thought with frustration, of all the things, tiny and big, that seemed to stop them from making any plans. She said nothing to Nan about it, and that was one more thing — the fact that all their plans and dreams were so nebulous that she could not announce them, could not expect the girls to take them seriously, had to move along as she was doing this year without any outward and visible confirmation of their love.

" What are you doing tonight? " Nan asked idly.

" Jack wants to go to a concert," Pat said. " I'm not sure whether it's settled or not. You know, he still likes you. He talks about you all the time when we're out together. I talk about Tim, and we cheer each other up."

" You're really serious about Tim, aren't you? " Nan asked curiously. " I don't get it. I mean, Tim is a nice boy, I guess. But you're so young — only in high school! I want to do a million things before I settle down."

" I don't," said Pat. " All I want to do is get married."

" When I get married, it's going to be to a man who has to travel," Nan announced.

" I'd like to travel," Pat agreed, suddenly remembering the world beyond her private little dreams. " But not without Tim."

" Did I tell you we might go to Florida this spring? "

" No! After Mexico at Christmas? "

Florida! The name conjured up for Pat the same kind of luxury and excitement that orchids did — more, in fact, than Mexico or Europe. It seemed as if Florida were the eventual ambition of her life, as an orchid was the immediate ambition, and she reflected with an irony she had never felt before on the unfairness of life that gave every-

79

thing Pat wanted to a girl named Nan.

Money is not important, Pat told herself firmly when she had left Nan and gone back home to a late, dull Saturday afternoon. But it seemed to invade every wish, every department of her life. She wanted to talk to Tim, but he didn't have a dollar to spend on a telephone call — and neither did she. She could not talk to her mother about expensive clothes and holiday trips. Mrs. Marlowe had repeated her philosophy too many times already: "Money is delightful when you have it — like curly hair or a talent for playing the piano by ear. If you haven't got it, there's no use complaining. You enjoy what you have."

Pat felt impatient at the thought of the words, but at the same time she tried to make of them a rock on which to stand. And then the telephone rang.

"Pat? Hi, darling. This is Tim."

"Tim!" she gasped. "How wonderful to hear from you! You don't know how much I've been missing you."

"Me too. That's why I called. I hoped I'd catch you home. Nothing much doing here, and I wanted to talk to you."

She told him about the party last night and shopping with Nan this afternoon, and listened to his story about a party he had attended last night with the boys. All too soon he said: "I'll have to ring off, darling. I'll call again and I'll write tomorrow."

But at least he had called. That wish had come true, and she gazed at the telephone with awe as she replaced it. It was less than two weeks now until he would be home for Thanksgiving.

Those two weeks went by quickly. Pat studied hard for exams, she tried out for a Christmas play and got a minor part, which meant lots of time in rehearsal, and she went out looking for a holiday job. To her astonishment, she got one at Sinclair's, because of her experience in selling at Baron's last year.

In a burst of purposeful planning she found her bankbook, put two dollars into her savings account, which brought it up to seventy-six dollars, and planned to save two hundred dollars by next summer. If she wanted to get married, she'd have to save a lot, she thought, feeling that now her plans were on a bedrock foundation.

And then it was Wednesday night, Tim came home, and it seemed again as if he'd never been away.

It was Friday night before they could have a long private talk together, what with eating Thanksgiving dinners apart with their own families, seeing friends who were home for the holidays, visiting Connie and Joanne, and then visiting the Marlowes and the Davises as a couple. But after what seemed like endless social responsibilities, they were alone at last, having a milkshake at the Cupboard.

Pat told Tim about Nan's party, which she had not had time to describe in detail before.

"It was so lush," she said yearningly. "I kept thinking of you and how much more fun it would have been with you there. Someday I hope we have piles of money, Tim. I want to go out to dine in evening dress and see another hit show from the tenth row —"

He grinned as if he didn't believe a word she said.

"It probably isn't going to happen that way with me," he said. "I don't ever expect to have that kind of money, and I don't even care."

"But, honey, you could have it if you wanted," Pat said.

"Anyone can make lots of money if he tries!"

"That's a fallacy," he said. "But I'm not even going to try."

She stared at him as if he were speaking Greek.

"Well, what else are you going to be doing?" she demanded. "If you have to make a living, why not make a good one? What are you going to do for a living?"

He shrugged. "I haven't decided yet," he said. "But lots of the things I'd like to do don't pay very much, and I'd rather enjoy the work than the salary."

"Well, yes," she agreed doubtfully. "Only it seems as if you could do both, like a girl falling in love with a millionaire."

"That's easier said than done too," he reminded her.

She laughed, remembering Nan's guests. "Those boys were wealthy, but that was one time when money seemed hardly worth it," she conceded. "But, Tim, did I tell you about Nan's orchid? It was the loveliest thing you ever saw. Someday I want you to give me one."

He reached across and held her hand.

"Someday I'll give you the moon with a crystal fence around it," he said. "But not this year. Orchids are out of my line, honey. I might as well tell you now. In fact, I've been telling you."

"I know," Pat said, because she did know. "Don't worry about it. But sometime — for some special reason."

"Sometime," he promised. "But don't hold your breath while you're waiting."

They talked about Christmas presents and agreed to spend not more than five dollars on each other, after some argument on Pat's part.

"But I've got this job," she protested. "I'm earning lots

82

of money, and if I want to spend more than that — "

"But I'm not earning that much," Tim pointed out, "and if I were, I'd want to save it for our bank account. It isn't the money, honey; it's the idea behind it."

"So it is," Pat agreed doubtfully. The words were familiar, but still they did not sound in her heart with conviction. And she could not reject the unwilling thought that five dollars bought hardly anything really worth having.

10

All the conversation in Nan's crowd during the weeks after Thanksgiving revolved about the glamorous trips the girls were taking during the Christmas holidays. Nan talked about Mexico. Marcia Pettit was going to California with her parents, flying both ways and spending the fortnight with friends in Pasadena, who were intimate friends of movie stars. Lynn was going to New York, and her parents already had tickets for three new shows, including one for which seats were sold out three months ahead. One of the other girls was going to Colorado for skiing; another was going on a West Indies cruise.

And Pat was going to get married, she told herself a little defiantly. Not right away, but at least it was a dream that could match these other dreams, and gave her a good reason for not traveling.

It was a good thing she was working at Sinclair's. Otherwise she would have been drawn into the shopping whirl the girls described so happily at lunch, and she was unhappy enough already without being exposed to the new clothes and accessories that she could not have. They told her she was lucky to have a job, and she knew she was. Jobs were not so easy to find as they had been a year or two ago. But she felt sure that they said to each other patronizingly: " The poor girl! She is lucky to have a job since she needs one," and she writhed under the idea of pity.

" Why do you see so much of these girls when they make you unhappy? " her mother asked once or twice when Pat was talking about all the things she could not have.

Pat said indignantly: " Why, they're some of my best friends! I'm crazy about them."

But she knew, even though it seemed unworthy of recognition, that there was a prestige about being part of " the crowd " that she enjoyed too much to give up. She enjoyed a heady measure of success in being on friendly terms with these girls, sitting with them at the football and basketball games, exchanging greetings in the school halls (aware of the freshmen and sophomores who eyed her with envy and admiration), greeting the parade of distinguished athletes, class officers, and student leaders who passed their table at lunch. She had never felt so important before, and her friendship with Nan and Nan's friends seemed to be the peak of success.

Like all success there were inherent drawbacks, and this baffled and confused her. When something was as satisfactory as her senior year was turning out to be, it seemed unfair to find frustrations growing like weeds among the satisfactions.

However, she concealed her discontent and told everyone brightly that she was terribly lucky, assured each traveler that she, Pat, envied her miserably, but that she herself couldn't leave town even if the chance came up because Tim would be here, and of course she couldn't be away from Tim during Christmas vacation.

Thus she matched prestige for prestige, since her romance bestowed upon her a distinction that even traveling (with one's family) did not bestow.

Unfortunately, even that distinction required the skill of a tightrope walker not to betray her into a morass of humiliation and condescending pity.

She could talk about Tim's telephone calls, letting them sound like daily instead of fortnightly events. She could talk about the daily letters, about the dance at Crandall next February, about the way he came home unexpectedly because he couldn't stay away from her another minute. But instinct warned her not to talk about their plans to get married, since Nan had implied weeks ago that she thought it was odd of a girl in high school to entertain such plans. And Pat could not, as the other girls did, talk about the Christmas presents they were exchanging, or the money he spent on her, or the new car he was about to buy.

Such conversations went on constantly, and daily she seemed to be fending, feinting, implying, concealing, covering up.

Like today, when Nan said: "Oh, I found the most terrific present for Dick! You know how fascinated he is with photography. Well, Daddy found this new light meter and said, why didn't I get it for Dick. It costs about thirty dollars, but it's a wonderful improvement, and I know he hasn't got one yet. So I'm terribly pleased with it. You know how hard men are to shop for."

"I know," Marcia agreed. "I'm absolutely baffled about Bill. I was all set to get him a new tennis racket — you know those championship rackets that came out this year? And doesn't he go and get it for himself just last week! "

"You might get him a second racket," Nan suggested.

"Or how about a new golf club? He plays golf so much."

"All his clubs are matched, and I don't think he needs a new one," Marcia sighed. "I can always get him a couple of dozen golf balls — but I must say that doesn't seem very inspired. What are you getting Tim, Pat?"

Fortunately Pat had already lifted her glass, and she took a long drink of milk while she marshaled her thoughts for a noncommittal reply. She couldn't tell the girls that Tim had insisted that they limit the cost of their presents to each other to five dollars apiece. And she didn't dare pretend she was giving him the kind of present they were giving their boy friends. They would be sure to find out after Christmas that all she had given him was a sport shirt, and a five-dollar one at that.

At last, setting down her glass, she said very casually: "I'm still trying to decide. I've thought of desk accessories, but I'm not sure of the color yet. Men *are* hard to shop for, aren't they?"

If she gave him only a letter opener, she thought with a sense of inspiration, it would be "desk accessories" after Christmas, and no one would know the difference.

"I don't want him to spend much on me," she went on seriously. "He's working his way through college and he doesn't have much money to spend."

She sounded proud of the fact that he had enough initiative and talent to work his way through college, and she hoped the girls would get the idea.

Marcia said: "Bill plans to earn lots of money in college with this dance band he belongs to. He wants to go to Europe every summer. I don't know when I'll see him after this year."

So there they were, back on travel again, with Bill earning unheard-of sums while going to school, and Pat subsided, listening with an uneasy sense of having shut a lot out of her life too soon.

That divided mind bothered her. She could feel resentment growing about not having as much money to spend as her friends, and probably not having much until she was so old it would no longer matter.

Even Jack Willis talked about traveling. He planned to go to Florida for spring vacation, he told her when he took her out on Friday night. One of his friends had a brother in college who was planning to drive to Florida, and the college men had agreed to take the high school boys along. He talked about the trip most of the evening, and went on from Florida to freighter trips, to Caribbean cruises, to trips around the world, spinning dream-colored fantasies around a life of roaming.

When he left he said: " I suppose I won't even see you till next year, with Tim at home. Have a merry Christmas."

" Same to you, Jack. Don't go around the world without telling me good-by."

She was smiling as she went about putting out the lights before she went upstairs. Jack was always fun, and she always had something to think about when they had been together. The dreams they had spun floated through her sleep, but in the morning when she recalled them all she could see was the money they would cost to realize.

" Sometimes I think money is terribly important," she said to her mother at breakfast the next morning before she went off to work at Sinclair's.

" It is," her mother agreed, " for many reasons."

" There are so many things I want," Pat brooded. " Tim ought to earn more. We're never going to have enough to get married on — or have fun with."

"I wouldn't worry about that for a while," her mother said, with that dry intonation that Pat hated.

She always felt when her mother spoke that way that Mrs. Marlowe never expected this marriage to take place, and Pat herself fought constantly the pessimistic conviction that if it didn't happen soon it might not happen at all. She dropped the subject of money and marriage and drank her morning cup of coffee in moody silence. The postman's ring was a welcome interruption, and she ran to pick up the mail.

"Just a lot of Christmas ads," she said, dropping a pile of envelopes before her mother. "And some of your magazines. I've got a letter from Mike."

She read it through silently before she shared it with her mother, having learned earlier that Mike frequently confided things to her in his letters that he didn't want his mother to hear about.

"When is he coming home?"

"Next Friday," Pat said, reading aloud. "He's driving back with a Chicago boy who's a sophomore — Larry Orchard. They're leaving Friday night and expect to drive straight through and get in some time Saturday."

"I wish he wouldn't," said Mrs. Marlowe intensely. "I hate the idea of driving for twenty hours or so without a break. And they'll try to make time and go too fast. Maybe if we wired him money for plane fare he'd fly instead."

"I don't think so," Pat read on to the bottom of the last page. "He says Larry is counting on him to be a passenger, and they're both going to save money this way. Three other boys from this area wanted to ride along, and Larry is taking two of them, but the other has already bought train tickets. I think Mike figures he can't change his plans now and disappoint Larry."

Mrs. Marlowe said no more, but she looked out of the window as if she would be fighting worry until Mike arrived.

The part of the letter Pat did not read aloud interested her more than the information about Mike's trip home.

"I'd like to see Connie," he wrote. "She hasn't written for a couple of weeks now. Do you suppose she'll have any dates left? See what you can do about Saturday night, and I'll do something for you sometime."

This was not the anguished cry that had pervaded earlier letters, but Pat felt that he had probably determined, since he was coming home within the week, not to say any more about Connie's defections in correspondence if he could just see her. Inwardly she boiled at Connie's attitude. But if Mike wanted a date, she would see what she could do.

She could not see Connie till late Sunday afternoon when Pat called Connie and asked if they could get together for a while.

"I'll be delighted to have you come over." Connie sounded as if she were talking between clenched teeth. "I had the most awful fight with Bob McDougal last night! I told him I never wanted to see him again, and he said he was going to call me this afternoon, so I want to be sure to be busy."

"What's all this about Bob McDougal?" Pat inquired, when they had secreted themselves behind the closed door of Connie's bedroom.

Connie tossed her head angrily.

"He's been badgering me to go steady for weeks," she said. "Absolutely nagging me, and I couldn't make up my

90

mind. After all, I felt I still owed Mike something — " She glanced at Mike's sister to see if Pat appreciated this sense of obligation. "But then I began to fall for Bob. I didn't intend to, but I couldn't seem to help myself. So last night I said maybe it would be a good idea after all to go steady. And then he tells me, *then* he tells me, ' After New Year's '! So I said, 'Why, Bob, love isn't the kind of thing you can put on a calendar.' And he looked kind of fussed and confused, the way boys do, and he says his mother has invited his aunt and cousin here for the holidays, and she expects him to look after Susie all the time she's here, and naturally take her to the dances and parties! And where does that leave me, right at Christmas time? I was so mad I could have killed him, and I told him I'd never speak to him again. *Never*."

"Well, I guess your Christmas worries are over," Pat said. "That's what I came over about. I had a letter from Mike yesterday. He says he hasn't heard from you for a couple of weeks."

She looked at Connie sternly, and Connie looked back at her with a skeptical expression.

"Mike wants a date for Saturday night when he gets home, if you've got any time," Pat said.

"I didn't know whether he was going to see me or not," Connie remarked. "Sure, I'll save Saturday night for him."

She sounded much too casual, and Pat wondered whether she was covering up excitement or whether she really didn't care.

"I don't think he's got a date for New Year's Eve, either," she said cautiously, not quite sure how far to carry Mike's request to ' see what you can do about Saturday.'

Connie shrugged, as if she did not care one way or the

other. "So far, it's open," she said. "Bob McDougal took care of that."

"Maybe we could double that night, the way we did last summer," Pat said, with a nostalgic wistfulness. It was tempting to go back to last summer when everything had looked so sure and golden, when no conflicting desires had entered her life, and when she had felt so certain of the pattern she planned.

"We'll do it," said Connie, looking for a moment more eager than she had any time since Mike had gone away.

11

Tim was coming home on Saturday before Christmas, and Pat could not see him until evening, because that was Sinclair's busiest day of the year. She told herself the time would pass more quickly when she was busy, and she could call him when she got home as if he had never been away. But it was not easy to concentrate at nine thirty in the morning, wondering how soon he would be in Allandale, thinking of all the things she wanted to tell him, remembering that on Monday, Christmas Eve, she would again have to spend the day at work. And in addition to all her other worries, she had not yet found his Christmas present.

She was working at the jewelry counter, and it seemed as if everyone in town wanted jewelry for Christmas.

" But I know you had it yesterday," a gray-haired matron in mink declared. " I asked the other girl here if you had plenty of those necklaces you advertised, and she said there were lots of them. And now you say they're all gone. Are you sure there isn't one tucked away under the counter somewhere? "

Pat ducked under the counter, looking through piles of

boxes for a necklace that was almost like the one on the counter but not quite, and she came up, hot and irritated, to control her tone of voice and assure the customer pleasantly: " I'm so sorry. We did have several yesterday afternoon, but I know they were selling fast. It was a very special value."

" I know it was," said the customer in annoyance. " That's why I want it. It wasn't returnable, so I had to ask my daughter-in-law first if it was what she wanted."

She fussed around looking at the other necklaces, asking Pat a question every two minutes, and decided after fifteen minutes that nothing else was as desirable as the one she couldn't have, so she left.

Two other women demanded Pat's attention at once, and when she turned to one of them, the other one said, " Well, I've been waiting for half an hour, and the meter is running out on my car. I'll have to let it go."

She went away, angry at the store and at Pat. The customer Pat was waiting on could not make up her mind for ten minutes, while others gathered and waited, and when she finally settled for some earrings at $1.19, she looked discontented over her selection.

It seemed as if the customers became more unreasonable as the Christmas deadline approached, and by the end of the day Pat's sales total was smaller than usual. She was exhausted, too exhausted even to care about calling Tim until she had soaked in a hot bath and stretched out on her bed for a few minutes. She had just laid down when the phone rang.

" Tim, darling, you're home! I'm so glad to hear from you. When can you come over? "

" I thought you were going to call me when you got

home." He sounded aggrieved. "I can't get there early tonight, Pat. Dad's stuck at the store. One of his clerks got sick yesterday, and the stock is in a mess. He has to work late to get the store ready for Monday, and he's counting on me to help."

"But, Tim!" she wailed. "You've been gone so long. I shouldn't think you'd have to work like that the minute you get home."

"It's something that goes with Christmas." He sounded more philosophical than she liked. "It's Dad's busiest season and I have to help out. I'll probably have to work part of Sunday too. But I'll be over around ten o'clock, if not before. O.K.? Don't be mad, darling, I can't help it."

"I'm not mad," she said, feeling very patient. "I can wait, I guess. Only I wish I didn't have to."

"I wish so too."

No sooner had she laid down than the telephone rang again, and knowing it wouldn't be Tim this time, she let her mother answer it. Five minutes later her mother knocked on her door and entered, her face white.

"That was a Gary hospital calling," she said. "Mike's had an accident. They said he's not hurt too badly, but he'll have to stay there for a while. Oh, I knew something like this would happen if he drove home!" She twisted her hands together as if it helped her to think. "Dad and I are going down there now, and I don't know when we can get back. You'll have to look after Denny, Pat. Now do please be careful and use good judgment."

Pat sat upright, her heart pounding.

"How did it happen? Who was driving?"

Her mother was holding her hands tightly together.

"I don't know any of the details," she said. "All I know

95

is that they said Mike has a broken arm, but no other injuries. I want to get there as soon as possible."

She went into her room and began packing a bag with quick nervous gestures. Pat lay back on her bed, thinking of Mike's accident, and calming herself fairly promptly with the reminder that a broken arm was not serious. The hospital said that was all —

The telephone rang again, and her mother called for Pat to answer. It was going on eight o'clock, and Connie wanted to know about Mike.

"I thought we had a date for tonight," she said to Pat as if she were prepared to be angry about it. "I haven't heard from him yet and I was beginning to wonder."

Pat explained the emergency, and then a thought occurred to her.

"Can you spend the night here? If you can, come along about eight thirty. I need your company, Connie! "

"I'll be there," Connie accepted promptly. "I'm terribly sorry about Mike. I do hope he's going to be able to come home for Christmas."

"We all do. But we don't know till Mother and Dad get down to the hospital to find out how he is. Tim is coming in around ten."

Mr. and Mrs. Marlowe departed, promising to call Pat from Gary as soon as they could tell her about Mike, and telling each other as they went out the door not to worry, that the hospital *said* he was all right. Connie arrived, in time to send a message to Mike, and the two girls settled down with soft drinks to pass the evening before a blazing fire. Denny, temporarily quenched by the possibility of serious trouble for his beloved older brother, withdrew to the TV room, where he stared fixedly at mystery programs

96

until midnight, when Pat belatedly remembered to send him to bed.

It had been a long time since Pat and Connie had spent an evening together, and they discovered much to talk over. Connie thought that Pat was going out a great deal with Jack Willis and was surprised when Pat assured her that Jack was just for fun. Connie was interested in Nan and her crowd, and inclined to feel that Pat had deserted other older friends for new ones. Pat assured her that she had not forgotten the old friends, meaning Connie, but she was working so hard with the drama department that she didn't seem to have much time for anyone these days. Pat felt that Connie was being unfaithful to Mike, and this was a good time to talk to her about it. Connie countered with the suggestion that there was not as much difference as Pat supposed between her own activities and Pat's.

"But Mike says you don't write very often," Pat accused her. "The poor boy is moping out there away from all his friends."

"He's not moping," Connie assured her crisply. "He's been dating a girl from Wellesley every weekend since Halloween. For the past six weeks every letter has been full of Kate and what she did and how well she dances. I didn't think it was very flattering, to be frank about it, and I lost interest in writing."

This was a new idea. Pat had gone along all fall believing that Mike was devoted singleheartedly to Connie. Now she remembered Gwen with a sinking feeling.

"Tim talks about a girl at Crandall too," she said, partly to share her anxiety with Connie, partly to let her know that all boys went out with other girls when they were away from the one they loved.

Connie looked at her sharply. "Are you still as much interested in Tim as ever?"

"Oh, definitely."

"I think it's a great mistake to make up your mind in high school. You have to give up so much that way."

"Oh, I don't know. It's not so different from going steady, except that we know it's for keeps."

"But it *is* different," Connie contradicted her, leaning forward in her conviction. "Going steady is fun — part of the time. But getting engaged and talking about getting married is a lot more than fun — it's a serious business. At least it ought to be."

"Certainly it's serious," Pat agreed. "That's the point."

Connie leaned back, shaking her head. "Well, of course, I never fell in love that way and I'm glad. I wouldn't have any sense of freedom."

"But you don't understand," Pat began, and then she stopped with a small secret smile. Those were the words she used to her mother, sure that parents never could understand their children. Now she remembered that Nan could not understand what love was like either, and here was Connie, her long-time friend. How could she explain?

Her mind ranged across the interwoven threads in her relationship with Tim: her friendship with his parents; her plans for college, still hinging on her plans with Tim; her bank account, growing for only one purpose; the months of time that had been woven into their lives; and most of all she thought of the way she knew Tim, his every gesture, his every mood, his likes and dislikes, his responsive affection, his quick humor. How could she ever get to know another man so well? She couldn't imagine loving anyone else.

98

"Maybe I don't understand," Connie acquiesced. "I never felt that way about anyone. I was thrilled about Mike last spring. But not that way! I'd be glad enough to go to a dance at Princeton, if he asked me, but not for love. I mean, I like him, but that's all. I like lots of boys and I'm having a wonderful time this year. I wouldn't want to shut it all off yet. You don't mean you want to get married soon and start in keeping house and doing laundry and cooking all the meals and all the things you'd have to do?"

"The sooner the better!"

Connie looked at Pat as if she had changed before her eyes.

"I don't get it," she murmured. "But Joanne was that way too."

"You fall in love when you meet the right man," Pat said, feeling that she was proclaiming eternal truths. "Some girls meet him in college, some in careers. I happened to meet Tim in high school, and I like it this way."

The doorbell rang and Pat sprang up. It was Tim, tall and handsome, covered with a light sprinkling of snow. As he swept her into his arms for a homecoming kiss Pat thought suddenly what fun to have Connie there. She could pretend for the space of an evening that she and Tim were entertaining in their own home.

She made cocoa and brought out a tray with cups and cookies on it. Tim leaned back in the big lounge chair and stretched his feet before him, looking at the fire, the drawn curtains, the pleasant lamp-lighted room, and sighed with pleasure.

"This is the life," he said happily. "What have you been doing since I was home last?"

She told him about Mike, about her job, very briefly, and then about the Christmas play at school, a miracle play done in the seventeenth-century manner, which she had found even more interesting to work in than *Good House-keeping*. Her growing enthusiasm for the theater had advanced strongly in that experience, and she looked forward with high anticipation to the winter play after vacation.

Somewhere in her story of what she had been doing she realized that Tim was listening only politely, without real interest, and with an almost unrecognized sense of disappointment, she cut off her enthusiasm and talked about her work at Sinclair's.

"Good girl," Tim said lazily. "I approve of working. How much money did you save?"

"Oh, quite a bit," Pat said vaguely. "Maybe fifty dollars. I'll deposit it the day after Christmas."

"But what on earth did you spend all the rest for?" Tim demanded.

She recoiled from his question. She had bought some new clothes — an expensive sweater to add to her wardrobe, which she felt she must build up before she got married, a skirt that had been a bargain at fifteen dollars because it was marked down from thirty. But she couldn't tell Tim about those things. He would think the prices were ridiculous, that she was extravagant beyond reason, that she didn't need clothes nearly as much as she needed money in the bank. She didn't want to tell him about the new clothes and yet she wanted him to know. Most of the pleasure in them would be gone if she couldn't share it with Tim.

There must be something wrong in their relationship, she thought, if she couldn't be frank about these things.

And yet, if she were frank, he would be critical, and which of them was right? She tightened her lips, determined that she was not going to argue about it.

The silence became demanding. She glanced up to meet Tim's eyes looking puzzled.

"Well," she said defiantly, "there were things I needed, and I got them with some of the money I earned."

There was another heavy silence. Tim drank some cocoa and stared into the fire broodingly. Pat knew what he was thinking: he wanted to assert some authority over the way she spent her money, he didn't approve of her extravagance, and he had said so before. But this time she was not going to accept any disagreement; she would tell him off if he tried to boss her around. And she knew that he knew how she felt and that he was trying to avoid argument in this their first meeting.

She sighed, wishing they didn't have these disagreements, sure that if they were married, understanding would be immediately simplified. Tim would understand what she needed.

"When we're married," Tim said slowly, "maybe you'll see what I mean."

He had taken the words from her own thought, and the coincidence seemed remarkable and symbolic. Her mood cleared, and she smiled at him with great sweetness.

"Honey, when we're married everything will be different," she said.

The telephone rang sharply, cutting through the quiet house with an urgent alarm. Pat sprang up.

"That must be the folks calling from the hospital," she said, running to the phone.

"Mike's going to be all right," she reported, returning

101

five minutes later with a sober expression. "The boy who was sitting next to the driver was killed! The driver is still unconscious and probably won't be able to leave the hospital for a week. But Mike can come home tomorrow. He's got a broken arm, but that's all."

"I'm very glad," said Connie sincerely. "Goodness, what a narrow escape! What happened?"

"They were hurrying, the way Mother was afraid they would, and this truck was stalled on the shoulder. The lights were flickering, but it was around a bend, and when the boys saw it they were almost on top of it. So they swerved to miss it and hit a patch of ice and smashed into a tree. Tim, I want you to use the train from now on."

"My drivers are as careful as I am," said Tim. "I wouldn't ride with them if they weren't."

The thread of the earlier conversation had been broken, and Pat was glad enough not to pick it up again. She refilled cocoa cups, passed cookies again, and they talked about all the things they had to do the last two days before Christmas.

Tim took his leave, promising to see her on Sunday. By the time she and Connie had washed up the cups and plates, remembered Denny, and gotten ready for bed, Pat had rearranged the implications of Tim's conversation to suit herself. All it took was time, she told herself; all she needed was this two-week holiday with Tim, and he would see her point of view. She especially wanted him to understand about travel, orchids, fine clothes — money.

It was important for them to plan their own life in that direction, and she felt, with a sense of maturity, that these were the years to make that plan.

12

On Monday, Christmas Eve, Pat had to find a present for Tim.

This problem had been on her mind since early in the month, and although she had talked about " desk accessories " because of the snob value in being able to tell her friends about them, she did not really want to give Tim anything so impersonal. Nor did she want to give him a sport shirt. That was the kind of thing he would buy for himself. She wanted something special, something personal, and her mind was a blank, especially when she remembered the five-dollar limit.

Just before her noon hour on Monday she remembered that his muffler was worn and old. A new muffler seemed unoriginal, but she was desperate now, and she arrived at Allandale's finest men's store at five minutes after twelve. Mufflers ranged from two dollars to ten dollars, and only one was exactly right: a fine soft flannel mixed with cashmere, in dark red. She chose it before she looked at the price, after discarding all the ten-dollar mufflers because the colors were wrong. When she found that her choice was exactly five dollars she was astounded. At first she thought it must be marked wrong. But the price was correctly marked. So it must prove that Tim had been right, she thought, smiling at the thought. It felt good to know that Tim was right even when she was not prepared to agree with him.

She bought the muffler, had it gift-wrapped, and carried it back to Sinclair's with a delightful sense of satisfaction. The more she thought about it, the better she liked her choice, until she was pleasantly convinced that if she had had thirty dollars to spend, she could not have found anything she would have liked better.

When she arrived home at six o'clock on Christmas Eve, dead-tired but buoyed up by her sense of accomplishment in having finished her Christmas shopping, she found Mike stretched out on the living room couch, pale and tired, his arm in a heavy cast supported by a sling.

"Well, Merry Christmas!" she said. "Brother, I'm glad to see you. It sounded like a narrow escape."

"Very narrow," he agreed. "I guess I was out for a couple of hours."

He seemed disinclined to talk about the crash, and his face was sober and old. He spent long stretches of time staring into the fire saying nothing and seemed to come back to his family with an air of bewilderment and surprise when anyone spoke to him.

"Let him alone," Mrs. Marlowe said to Pat in the kitchen in a low voice. "Knowing that one of the boys was killed, was a terrible shock to him. It was Doug Campbell, one of his best friends at school. He met Doug on the train last fall and has liked him ever since. Let him talk when he feels like it, and be quiet when he wants to be."

Pat remembered the smiling youth who had stood next

to Mike to wave good-by to his own parents through the train window. She was stunned. Death seemed so much closer when it happened to someone you knew, even as slightly as she knew Doug Campbell.

"Mike was lucky," she said soberly.

"*We* were lucky," her mother said. "I feel so bad about the Campbells. We met them at the hospital."

Even Denny was sobered by his big brother's narrow escape. He said brusquely, when Mrs. Marlowe repeated her warning, "I know, I know. I won't bother him."

Mike wanted to get to bed, he told his father shortly after dinner. He had been too tired to climb the stairs when he came in, but now he thought he could make it. So he went off, walking heavily as if each step cost him an effort, and hauling himself up the stairs by the rail. His father helped him to get undressed and into bed.

"At least he'll go back on the train," her mother told Pat. "And the doctor says his arm will be back in use in six weeks or so. I hope it doesn't interfere with his plans for the rest of the year or with his studying."

"I should think he could study even with a broken arm."

"He could study as far as the arm is concerned," Mrs. Marlowe said, looking disturbed. "But he's so upset about Doug he acts as if he's in a fog most of the time. When he gets back to school and misses Doug at every turn, I don't know what it will do to him."

Connie called to inquire about Mike, and Pat explained that it seemed more serious than she had expected. She promised Connie that Mike would call her when he felt up to talking on the telephone and hung up, wondering how Connie would take this development. Last year when Mike had suffered injuries in football Connie had sat by the couch for hours and visited with him. But that was last year and long ago.

When Tim arrived Denny said, "Hiya," and unexpectedly thrust out his hand. Pat was delighted. Last year Denny had been a noisy little show-off, constantly embarrassing her and making awkward remarks at the wrong time. This year, almost twelve years old, he seemed to want to act more like a man of the world than a small boy. She wanted to hug him, in one of her rare moments of affection for her small brother.

They all sat around the fire, and Tim told them about the Valentine formal for which the date had just been set. He wanted Pat to come to the college for the dance. Her father and mother agreed that it sounded delightful, and Pat listened to the discussion of trains, sleeping in the girls' dorm, where she would take her meals, with a pounding heart. Her first college dance! It seemed impossibly exciting, and she thought she could never live until that weekend came around.

"What are you planning to major in?" Mr. Marlowe asked Tim abruptly. "Got any ideas yet?"

Tim sat up a little self-consciously.

"I didn't know what I wanted when I got there," he said. "But I've been giving it a lot of thought since then and I think I'm going to major in math. It's my favorite subject."

"Lots of openings for math majors," Mr. Marlowe agreed. "Going into business?"

"I haven't entirely decided yet," Tim said. "I may want to do graduate work. I might even like to teach."

"Teachers are certainly needed," Mrs. Marlowe said, laying down the jacket she was mending for Denny. "I think that would be a wonderful profession, Tim."

He looked pleased with their approval, and his eyes went from them to Pat. But she was looking into the fire, steadily averting her face from his, undecided what reaction she was going to have to his announcement. More years of study, less money — what would such an idea do to their plans for getting married? And what college professor could ever buy orchids for his wife?

"Of course," he said, as if he were trying to conceal nothing about his future, "there isn't much money in teaching. But that isn't the important thing."

Pat raised her head protestingly and then kept silent. Even with her conviction that luxury was everyone's right if he wanted it badly enough, she knew that this was not an admirable argument. Admirable or not, that was the way she felt, she thought, setting her jaw stubbornly.

Mrs. Marlowe went upstairs to see if Mike needed anything. Mr. Marlowe reminded everyone that tomorrow was Christmas. Tim asked if Pat could drive over to his house to say Merry Christmas to his parents.

She wanted to give Tim his present that night, partly because she was so pleased with it, partly because she knew that tomorrow would be confused with people, other presents, and family obligations, and she wanted Tim's present to be important all by itself.

"I've got your Christmas present with me," she said, as they stopped in front of his house. "Why don't I give it to you while we are all by ourselves?"

"That's what I'd like," he said. "I've got yours too. But in front of the whole family it seemed like having too much of an audience."

He pulled a tiny box out of his pocket, and she handed

him her package wrapped in shining silver paper with a scarlet ribbon. Pat took the tiny box he gave her, wondering what he had thought of. He waited for her to open it.

"Tim!" she gasped. "How lovely!"

She took out of the box a hand-wrought silver ring twisted in a lover's-knot design, with their two names engraved on it, and held it up. Tim slipped it on her fourth finger.

"To show this place is reserved for a diamond," he said with a kiss. "Do you really like it? A jeweler near Crandall designs and makes his own jewelry, and he made this just for you."

"But you spent more than five dollars!"

"Well, yes," he admitted. "But what's a little money when I find exactly what I want you to have?"

"You darling! Oh, I hope you like your present as much as I love this one!"

He opened the box, tearing off the red ribbon and silver paper as if he didn't notice the wrapping.

"Say!" He lifted out the dark-red muffler. "You've got taste, girl. This is nicer than anything I've ever worn!"

"I'm so glad," she said intensely. "I liked it the minute I saw it." Her fingers met his as he rubbed the scarf against his cheek, enjoying the fine, silky wool.

She knew that he was as pleased with her present as she was with his, and her heart sang. Nothing was as truly gratifying, she thought with the excitement of a new discovery, as to give the one you loved something he truly enjoyed. And she realized that the cost was the least important thing about either gift. It would be more pleasure to show her ring to the girls than to talk about a cashmere sweater.

Some understanding of the meaning of money in her life was beginning to dawn, faint as yet, hardly recognizable, but still the first suggestion of a new pattern of thought.

⚜

On Christmas afternoon Connie came over to see Mike. She conferred with Pat in whispered tones at the door for a minute.

"How's he feeling?"

"Pretty good. But the depression is the worst of it."

Connie's eyes showed a concern that she had suppressed since Mike's departure for college in September.

"I did want to see him," she said, "and I brought him a present just for fun."

"He'll be awfully glad to see you," Pat assured her. She took Connie into the living room. "Mike, you've got a visitor."

Mike got to his feet slowly as if it were a great effort.

"Hiya, Connie! Glad to see you."

"Merry Christmas," Connie said, and she went over and kissed him. "I brought you a gimmick," she said laughing. "I wasn't going to embarrass you with a real present and then I saw this."

She tossed him the package, and he unwrapped it clumsily but expectantly and took out a small furry mechanical bear.

"Remember when we went to the zoo last summer?" Connie said nostalgically. "You liked the bears so much we stayed by their cage for half an hour."

She wound up the tiny bear and set it on the coffee table where it moved forward, swinging its head from side to side while the whole family watched, laughing.

"That's wonderful!" Mike leaned back, and already

some of the lines about his mouth had softened. " How've you been, you delinquent correspondent? "

He looked, Pat thought, as if he were forgetting the accident for the first time since he had been home.

"If you and Tim want a game of bridge this week " — Connie glanced at Pat — " we could still take you on. New Year's Eve we could play all night."

Mike's eyes brightened. He loved bridge.

" I didn't think you'd have any dates left by the time I pulled into town with this handicap." He indicated his cast.

"I've got plenty of dates left," Connie said. "A complete program for your vacation — entertainment, food, and diversion."

He grinned with pleasure, but his eyes showed more than pleasure. He was touched by her solicitude and he still cared as much as he had last fall.

Pat wondered how much it meant to Connie. But when she tried to find out, all Connie would say was: " I like Mike. I always have. But I want him to be free to roam and I want to be free myself. Why can't we have fun like this with no strings? "

Why not? Pat asked herself as the holiday went by.

But whatever answer seemed to work for Connie, Pat could not apply it to her own situation. She had no goal, as she had so truly told Tim, but to get married. So why look further? Some instinct warned her that there might be aspects of the question that she had overlooked, and she talked to her mother about it, not to ask for advice or reveal any possible doubt, but rather to confirm her determination by announcing it.

" I'd like to get married next summer," she remarked the week after Christmas, as she got out the vacuum cleaner to pick up fallen needles from under the tree.

Mrs. Marlowe looked up from the letter she was reading. "Why?"

"Oh, Mother, why not? I'll be eighteen, Tim will be a sophomore — We're adult, we know what we want. And this waiting is such a gap in our lives."

Mrs. Marlowe laid down her letter and looked at her daughter intently.

"There are lots of reasons not to marry so soon," she said. Pat listened, inwardly defying her mother to persuade her. "For one thing, you have nothing yet to contribute to a marriage and a family. You are not educated, in spite of a good high school. I mean, what the high school has tried to give you hasn't made much impression — because of your youth. For another reason, Tim is a serious-minded boy with a purpose, and he should have a chance to work toward that purpose without the complications of earning a living for a family and being involved with a wife."

Pat was listening in spite of herself, and her mother's words were sinking in, even as she tried to reject them.

"For another reason, there is no hurry. When you feel as if you can't wait another minute to get married, that's the very time to slow down and take a long look. After all, this will be for the rest of your life, not to pass the time for a year or two."

Pat pushed the vacuum cleaner slowly back and forth, thinking over her mother's words. She had to admit that they made sense. But the reasons did not seem to apply to Pat's own romance. Her love was different. She and Tim were different, and ordinary laws were not for them.

She said to her mother: "I can't see why Tim wouldn't

111

work even better at his studies when he's settled, and maybe college would mean more to me if I were married. Anyway, we'll talk it over."

She was astonished when she talked to Tim to discover that he felt somewhat as her mother did.

"But, darling," she cried, "I thought if we didn't have to be separated, it would be so much simpler."

"In lots of ways," he said, kissing her hungrily. "But I feel that when we get married I want to be able to take care of you, and I couldn't do that by next summer."

"Money!" Pat snapped her fingers. At this moment money did not matter; luxuries were unimportant. "We can work that out all right." She jotted down hasty figures and frowned at them. "It does cost a lot. But I'll save my money. I'll really save! And we can tell the folks at Easter how we're planning things."

"We might know better by Easter," he agreed.

13

T^{im} went back to Crandall on Sunday afternoon, and Pat went down to the station with his parents and watched him go out of her life again, wanting to cry and not allowing herself to give way because it seemed foolish to cry over leave-taking so often. She promised to see him for the February formal, and wondered forlornly how she would pass the six empty weeks before that happy date.

She rode home with Mr. and Mrs. Davis, chatting lightly about all the subjects Mrs. Davis raised, answering polite questions about her senior year, agreeing with them that Tim hated to leave and that it would seem like a long time before he returned.

"But I know you'll be busy," said Mrs. Davis comfortingly.

"Oh, sure."

Pat's thoughts turned to being busy: the speech department at the high school was casting a new play as soon as school opened, and she looked forward to working with it. She had not thought about the theater much since the Christmas play; busy with her job at Sinclair's and with Tim for two weeks, she had taken no time to look forward

113

to the new year at school, thinking only of next summer and getting married after graduation.

Now she remembered the heart-lifting excitement, the fast-paced activity behind the scenes, the deep satisfaction she found in the companionship of the congenial, single-minded group who worked with the plays, and she could hardly wait to get back to school.

The play for the winter quarter was going to be *The Taming of the Shrew.*

Pat glanced around the auditorium at the group who came in for auditions. Jack Willis was there, but Nan and the " big crowd " were missing. Nan told Pat at lunch time that she didn't think Shakespeare was worth the time it would take.

Shakespeare was reputed to be dull, and Pat herself could not feel excited about this choice. The only reason she came to audition was because any play was more exciting than anything else going on. And she found, as the auditions went on, that the different styles of reading and interpretation were engrossing, that there were some outstanding actors who had not appeared for *Good House-keeping.* When Jack whispered to her that Willa Sanders was a really gifted actress, the choice of leads became as exciting as a race. And the director was new, Mr. Bigelow.

The thing that made the theater exciting, Pat realized in this play, was watching someone like Willa Sanders, who was not suited to light comedy like *Good Housekeeping,* take a part like Kate in the *Shrew* and make her a lively contemporary person a little bigger than life. It was watching Mr. Bigelow refine Kate to a performance as good as the professional one Pat saw on television one

Sunday afternoon. It was watching him invent and build into the acting the subtle turns of characterization, the unexpected accents, the creative detail that polished the play into a performance beyond any expectation from a high school cast. It was discovering that Shakespeare offered more to work with, more material for creative satisfaction, than anything Pat had ever dreamed of.

In a letter to Tim after a fortnight of rehearsal she wrote in genuine astonishment and some dismay: "Don't you like Shakespeare? This is the most exciting thing I've ever done. Wait till you see a play sometime and you'll see what I mean."

Pat had a small part with only a dozen lines. But she worked on those lines, and Mr. Bigelow worked with her, as hard as Willa worked over Kate's part, and she discovered through her effort the music that came out of even unimportant lines. She was glad her part was small: it left her free to concentrate on the rest of the play, which had a changing fascination at every rehearsal. In the end she did not believe that anyone could see the play without appreciating it as she did, and conversely that no one could really appreciate it without having worked through it with Mr. Bigelow.

Toward the end of rehearsals Mr. Bigelow told them about the Northwestern Theater at the university in the next suburb. Season tickets for four plays were six dollars, and they would see not only different and very interesting plays, he told them, but some outstanding performances. He brought announcements of the productions and offered to buy tickets in a block for those who were interested.

Pat was enthralled. She was so deeply interested now

that it seemed as if she could hardly live long enough to see all the plays she wanted to see. She debated for five minutes whether to spend her six dollars or to put the money in her bank account for her marriage, and then unhesitatingly she bought the tickets. This was more important than anything else.

Six of the cast bought tickets together for Saturday nights: Pat and Jack Willis, Ron Flower and Willa Sanders, who were Petruchio and Kate, and Bob Kent and Marge Wilder, who were Lucentio and Bianca. Pat looked forward so much to seeing the plays at the university theater that she forgot about Tim for days at a time.

When she thought of him she felt guilty that she was not more unhappy about his absence, and she begged Tim to come home if he possibly could for the production of the *Shrew* the first week in February. When he wrote that he couldn't come home again before spring vacation, she was almost relieved. Remembering the cast party which would follow the *Shrew*, she realized that perhaps the weekend would be more fun without Tim.

The production went off with great acclaim. Everyone played at the peak of his ability; the whole cast felt, tinglingly, that *The Taming of the Shrew* had been the best play the high school had produced in several years; the audience was astounded at the virtuosity of the production, and the principal came backstage to commend the cast individually.

Afterward Pat went to the party with Jack Willis. And Jack was sparkling tonight with his own excitement for the play. But something new had been added: he expected more from Pat.

The evening was half over when she realized that all the

116

time he had been holding the floor, taking off Mr. Bigelow in a tense moment, taking off Ron's Petruchio, doing a clowning imitation of Kate, and keeping everyone laughing, all that time he kept watching for Pat's personal response.

For the first time Pat didn't find him as funny as usual. She laughed to be polite and drifted away from the circle around Jack to chat with a group in the other room around Mr. Bigelow. Half an hour later Jack joined her, looking offended.

"What's going on out here?" he inquired with great indifference. Then taking her arm he said: "Come on over to the piano, Pat. We're doing the *Kiss Me, Kate* songs again."

Jack had a fine strong tenor that had sounded above the group when they had sung the songs earlier in the evening, and Pat had a feeling that he wanted someone — her, if no one else would do it — to clamor for him to sing a solo. Perversely she refused to oblige him.

"I heard the songs," she said, pulling away from him. "I don't want to go over to the piano. I want to listen to what Mr. Bigelow is saying."

Jack looked hurt and then annoyed, and when she refused to join his audience at the piano he found Willa, whom he had told Pat he didn't like much, and persuaded her to sing a duet with him.

Watching him from the other room, as his voice sounded clearly and demandingly, Pat thought unexpectedly: "No wonder Tim doesn't like Jack. He was smart to spot his temperament so quickly."

For the rest of the evening Jack paid devoted attention to Willa until it was time to take Pat home.

"What was wrong with you tonight?" he demanded, as they drove toward her house. "You sure weren't as much fun as usual."

It was on the tip of her tongue to inquire caustically, "You mean, because I didn't want to watch you all evening?" and she bit it back, not really wanting to hurt him.

"I'm sorry," she said noncommittally. "Didn't you have fun anyway?"

"Oh, I don't know," he said in a dissatisfied tone. "Not as much as some of the other times. Maybe it's the letdown."

"We've all been working at a pretty high pitch," she agreed with him. "Thanks so much for bringing me home, Jack."

She was getting out of the car when he came around and joined her to walk up to the door in sad silence.

"Better luck next time." She tried to tease him into a smile.

"Not for me," he said forlornly. "My luck is so bad it's hopeless."

"Why, Jack, nobody's luck is that bad!"

"Mine is," he insisted, scuffing his toe across a patch of rough ice on the porch and watching it disintegrate. "Like with you — what good does it do me to fall for a girl who's got somebody else?"

"But, Jack!" Pat sounded astounded, but she was not really surprised. She had seen this coming. "I thought it was still Nan for you."

He shrugged. "I got over Nan last fall. Oh, well —" he sounded resigned to a life of tragedy. "Hear you're going to visit Tim next week. Have fun, Pat, and don't try to think of me."

118

He left her, striding manfully away, and she stared after him with her mouth open. The star in a homemade drama, she thought impatiently — the spotlight performer. She opened the door and went inside.

And yet, he could be such fun when he wasn't being self-centered. The self-centeredness had been growing, she realized, looking back over the *Shrew* rehearsals.

Suddenly she forgot all about Jack and his problems. She realized with the sensation of seeing a light appear to guide her steps in a wilderness, that she had found her goal in these past weeks, the purpose for which she had been looking more or less consciously ever since Mrs. Stevens had told her high school audience long ago that everyone needed a goal. Pat's goal was the theater.

She didn't have to act, she told herself, as she got ready for bed, although that was the " fun " part. But she wanted to work with acting and producing. It could be television, Broadway, " little theater," Hollywood, or teaching school, as Mr. Bigelow was doing so well. Money didn't matter.

She repeated that thought in astonishment, as she recognized the importance of what she had just let cross her mind. *Money didn't matter!* Now she knew why Tim said that about his work. When you knew what you really wanted to do, money was no longer important. She felt as if she had cast off a chain she had not even known she wore.

The main thing now, she thought as she turned out her light, was to get prepared for the kind of work she wanted to do. College was important for the first time in her life.

Sunday evening she lay down on her bed to think, her hands clasped under her head, staring at the ceiling and dreaming the bright dreams of success. She recalled the

119

delights of the *Shrew* production, regretful that it was over, exhilarated with the discovery of her goal, and projecting her dreams into a distant future until she was rigid with anticipation. The telephone rang, and she didn't even hear it.

"Pat," her mother called from downstairs, "Pat! Telephone."

Recalled to the present, Pat jumped to her feet with the startled sensation of being transported from a great distance.

"Hi, darling! How was the play?"

Tim was calling her from Crandall.

"Tim, darling! How wonderful to hear from you! The play was terrific. I would even have given up the cast party if you could have been here." The words were automatic, and she wondered, as if she stood apart from herself listening, how much she meant what she said.

Tim laughed. "I appreciate that, honey. I would even have gone to the cast party if I could have come home. I've been missing you so much this weekend I wanted to talk to you."

"I've been missing you too," Pat said, entirely truthfully. At the sound of his voice she was again achingly alone without him. "Mother is letting me leave school at noon Friday so the weekend can be a little longer. There's so much to tell you."

"You sound as if you've been having a gay time."

"Not gay, exactly. But this play was so tremendous. I do wish you could have seen it."

"I'm glad it was good. But Shakespeare isn't my dish."

"You would have liked this," she insisted.

"If you say so," he assented. "I'll see you Friday then.

The train gets in around nine, and I'll be there. It'll be a wonderful weekend."

She stood by the telephone a moment trying to reconcile the excitement of Tim's call with the dreams it had interrupted. Then slowly she went back to her bedroom and lay down again, thinking deeply. The mood of the dream was broken, but she could recall how she had felt fifteen minutes ago. And the dance at Crandall seemed less important now than when they had talked about it during Christmas vacation. Now it seemed little more than another date, and already her thoughts ranged beyond that weekend to the plans for the next play.

Some unexpected force had shaken up her life and emotions, and she was going to have to figure out all over again things she had thought were settled and final, a love she had been convinced solved everything and was all she wanted.

She loved Tim as much as ever, she told herself. The problem was in fitting this personal ambition into her life along with Tim. A month ago she had been convinced that there was nothing worth doing except getting married. Now she had found a purpose that was almost equally important.

She glanced at her watch: nine o'clock and Maurice Evans was on TV with his own interpretation of the *Shrew*. She switched off her problems and went down to watch Maurice Evans.

14

Keyed up, after all, with the excitement of her first college weekend, Pat sat rigidly on the dark-red mohair seat of the train and smiled through the window at her mother and father and Denny waiting on the platform for the train to pull out. Denny kept shouting things she could not understand. Her mother mouthed carefully, "Have a wonderful time!" Her father grinned and waved his newspaper as if this were the last good-by. But it was not. The train would not leave for five minutes yet.

Pat looked in the mirror between the windows, rearranged her hair, and discovered that her bags were not with her. With an expression of horror she turned to the window and gestured frantically toward the porters still trundling baggage to and fro. Her mother looked alarmed. Her father waved reassurance. Pat turned to the aisle and hurried toward the door where she could cry to them to find her bags. Without luggage she would have no clothes for the whole weekend!

Her way was blocked by a porter bringing in other people's bags, and she waited for him to get out of the way, noticing with mounting distress that her bags were not among those he carried. When she reached the open door the conductor was already waving all aboard to the engineer.

"But my bags aren't here!" Pat cried desperately.

He did not seem to hear her, and the wheels began to move. She darted back to her seat again, and already the window had slid past her waiting family. Squeezed against the pane of glass, she tried to wave one last time as they disappeared from sight. She could not tell whether they saw her or not, and she turned away from the window feeling that after days and weeks of anticipation everything was going wrong after all. And there were the bags, tucked neatly under the seat!

She stared at them incredulously and began to smile. "Where did you come from?" she muttered.

She could relax now. The train was gathering momentum, running smoothly above city streets, between apartment buildings where people leaned on window sills to watch it pass, where children stared and waved, swerving east to bring the lake into view again, and then settling down to a flying progress across open country.

Pat leaned her head against the cushion and let the rolling fields, the sand dunes, the sweeping highways pass her eyes. She was going to see Tim within a few hours, and the novelty of being with him like this, away from home, swept over her in a warm flood of happiness. She wanted to meet all his friends, to see the buildings where he had his classes, to visit the Shanty where all the students, he had told her, spent every evening over coffee or Cokes. But most of all she wanted to see Gwen, who filled some of Tim's empty hours, and whom she considered a serious threat. Gwen was to be her hostess in the girls' dormitory, which seemed to Pat, in spite of her

123

mother's question about it, entirely reasonable.

"After all, Gwen and I have a lot in common," she had explained to her mother. "We're both interested in Tim."

"I can imagine," her mother had agreed dryly. "But how is Gwen going to feel about Tim's taking you to this dance?"

"Oh, she won't mind," Pat asserted confidently. "She's going with somebody else. It isn't as if she wouldn't get there."

She wondered now if this occasion was as momentous to Tim as it seemed to her, and she thought again, as she had thought ever since the details had been arranged, that it would be a wonderful time for Tim to give her an orchid — her first orchid, to celebrate her first college dance, to signify the importance of her traveling to Crandall, of their being together at Crandall instead of at home. She hoped he would think of it, hoped prayerfully that their love was strong enough for her thoughts to be thus transmitted.

She watched the changing scene outside the window until dusk dimmed it. Then she went into the diner, feeling very mature to be ordering and eating alone, her eyes still following the fading landscape. When she had finished dinner, she went on to the club car and read a magazine. The other passengers, to her disappointment, all seemed to be elderly businessmen. There was not a college boy on the train.

The train stopped occasionally, and now and again she could distinguish faces in the glow of the station lights. The towns were small, and red lights glared, bells rang, and gates lowered across roadways as the train sped through. The sense of being far from her old life in time as

124

well as space was delicious. Even her newly discovered goal of the theater was something that belonged in Allendale with the rest of her life there. This weekend, Tim was more important.

The lights of Cincinnati blazed like earthbound stars; the train sped into the town, slowed down for the station, crawled into place, stopped. Pat put on her coat and stood endlessly in line behind people who seemed to be frozen in her path. At last she was standing on the step, and the waiting hand of the conductor helped her down. And there was Tim, looking as if he had been waiting all his life.

And now everything came into focus: she was here with Tim; the weekend was about to begin; everything was going to be perfect. They rode to Crandall, half an hour from Cincinnati by bus, and Tim seemed even more happy to have her there than she was to be with him. He took her to the dorm to leave her bags, and she met Gwen, who was alarmingly attractive, blond, perky, and sharp-eyed.

"Come on, Gwen," urged Tim. "Let's all go out and have coffee."

Gwen glanced at Pat and said: "I'm glad to meet you, Pat. I've been kind of curious to see you. It'll be fun to get acquainted this weekend." To Tim she said: "Thanks just the same, Tim, but I think I won't go out tonight. You show Pat all the things you want her to see, and don't forget that twelve o'clock sharp is the deadline for Friday night."

They went to the Shanty where Pat met Tim's roommate who was a great practical joker. She listened to students from Tim's math class exchange comments about the professor. She met a girl from Tim's Spanish class with whom Tim conversed fluently in Spanish. He enjoyed speaking the language, and Pat determined that she must take it in college.

"Some Spanish majors are taking the winter quarter down in Mexico City at the University of Mexico," he said. "Fun?"

"It would be terrific," Pat said, wondering what Spanish theater would be like.

On the way home he said longingly, "If we were married, it would be even more fun to go to the University of Mexico."

"It would be heavenly," she said, forgetting in the emotion of the moment any alternatives.

All the hopes and anticipation of early marriage invaded her thoughts again. She had had coffee at the Shanty and she could not sleep even after an hour's conversation with Gwen, who told her how wonderful Tim was, how much time they spent together, and repeated that she knew he belonged to Pat and she hoped Pat realized what a wonderful guy she'd caught.

"Oh, I know all right," Pat said. Then she added, with calculated emphasis, "That's why I'm going to marry him."

"If he were mine," Gwen said, "I wouldn't let him out alone. That boy needs a girl."

Pat did know, and the knowledge disturbed her. In the strange bed she turned and twisted, trying to fall asleep, aware that without sleep she was going to look bedraggled tomorrow, and then giving up the futile effort and letting her mind stray where it would.

If they could be married next summer, she kept thinking, they could travel together, they could go to college together, they would never have to be separated again. She planned details of their life together, china patterns, silver, the kind of furniture they would have, where the money would come from. In the dim, silent hours of the morning most of the answers seemed easy, and she skipped from one plan to another until she finally fell asleep and dreamed she was playing Kate to Tim's Petruchio. He performed the role with great flair, she noted with no surprise in her dream.

In the morning the dream recurred, and she thought wistfully how wonderful if it could be true, if she and Tim could enjoy the theater together.

He called for her at nine o'clock to take her out to breakfast. The campus was covered with snow that had fallen in the night, and seemed filled with the atmosphere of celebration attending the weekend festivities. The dream evaporated. Tim and the theater were hard now to think of together.

" I want to show you the campus this morning," he said. " The library is nice here — and the new classroom building. Then we're going downtown for lunch. This afternoon there's a swimming meet and an open house for visiting students. Then I want a couple of hours alone — " He grinned at her slyly, and she knew that he wanted to get her a valentine. " What color is your dress tonight? "

An orchid leaped immediately to her mind again, and she dwelt on the idea a moment to give it a chance to transfer to Tim's thoughts.

" I've got a new dress. It's pink, and something white would be good with it." Then she added, hoping his mind would take the same channel hers was taking: " Don't get me a valentine, Tim. Being down here is enough. Let the

— corsage — be the valentine." To herself she thought again intensely, Let it be an orchid!

" O. K., I'll figure something out," he said casually, as if he had already forgotten what they were talking about. " Ready to go and see some sights? "

She thought the campus was beautiful. The town of Crandall was small and charming. But she felt as if she had walked miles and been there a week by the end of the afternoon when she went back to the dorm to dress for the visiting students' reception.

The party was being given by the senior girls, and everyone wore a red heart with his name on it for identification. The refreshments were heart-shaped cookies and red fruit punch, and Pat met everyone on campus. Most of the guests seemed to know each other, including Tim who was enjoying himself talking to dozens of people.

Pat was enchanted for the first half hour and then after that she made an effort to enjoy herself. But the effort grew more and more difficult. When she didn't know any of the people, it was hard to enter into the conversations with enthusiasm or even to listen with interest. She and Tim approached one group who were talking about the spring play, a student talent show that was being auditioned and cast next week. Speculation on whether Irene would try out with her monologue, how a barbershop trio would fare with all the competition in harmony, whether it was true that the man and woman student directors had quarreled so bitterly as to be unable to work together, rumors about the lack of musical talent this year, rumors about theater scouts expected to attend the dress rehearsal: all these matters were of vital interest to the group around Pat, and Tim seemed as much interested as

128

the rest of them, since he knew all the people involved.

Pat listened, trying to be fascinated too, and remembering how exciting *The Taming of the Shrew* had been only last week. But the more she heard, the less sense it made, even after Tim pointed out Nicky across the room and Serena in another corner and identified them as the quarreling directors.

When it was time to go back to the dorm and get ready for dinner, Pat wondered what was wrong with her. She had never before failed to enjoy a large party. But Tim had always been unable to do so, she remembered with surprise. It was one of the things on which they differed, and she had accused him of being that way on purpose. With astonished realization she could understand him now: when she had dragged him to that cast party last fall, he had known no more of the other guests than she knew today. Poor boy, she thought fondly, no wonder he didn't have a good time. Now she knew how he felt.

It seemed as if she had climbed a long way toward solving some of their difficulties, and the thought filled her with fresh energy. She was tired no longer, but anxious to see Tim again. It was Valentine's Day, she remembered, and he was bringing her a valentine. She scrambled through a hurried shower and skipped back to Gwen's room as fast as she could.

Gwen was finishing a manicure that looked expert.

"Can I lend you anything?" she inquired, looking up as Pat came in wrapped in a towel. "I mean, if you find you've got a run or forgot an earring, let me know."

"Thanks a lot"—Pat began dressing—"but I think everything is in order." She had a feeling that Gwen was never going to be fond of her. It was too bad in a way, because she could have liked Gwen if it weren't for Tim.

"Did Tim ever tell you about the night we went up to the Crossroads Inn?" Gwen inquired with a little smile as if she were reliving secret memories.

"No, he didn't mention it," Pat said, wondering immediately why he hadn't. Gwen looked dreamy.

"It was the most divine night," she recounted. "Last fall — full moon — we were double-dating with another couple who had a car."

Gwen smiled again as if to herself. "I was ready to fall for him that night," she said. "We had a wonderful dinner and then we rode around and finally parked on a hilltop where we could see for miles in the moonlight. I'll never forget that night."

I'll bet she won't, Pat thought to herself, brushing her hair with an angry motion and glaring into the mirror. Aloud she said, "Was that before he came home in October?"

Gwen glanced up quickly. "Just before — or maybe afterward," she said smoothly. "When was it he came home?"

"Toward the end of October," said Pat. Not for anything would she reveal any detail of that happy weekend. She remembered the way they had spent Sunday riding through the fallen leaves —

"I don't remember exactly," Gwen shrugged. "There were so many times —"

Pat laid down her brush. "You mean full moon, week after week?"

"Oh, the moon doesn't have to be full," Gwen said sweetly. "It's pretty nice when it's dark and starlit too. It was touch and go for me for a while. And then I met

130

Clyde and realized that it was only a false alarm about Tim after all. I'm afraid he was a little upset."

She turned toward the closet to bring out her dress, and Pat stared at the back of her yellow head, burning with hatred. She seized her hairbrush and began brushing again, counting strokes so that she would not have to recall Gwen's words.

"You're going with Clyde tonight?" she asked, at the end of a hundred strokes.

Gwen shook out the crisp scarlet underskirt and settled the full overskirt above it. It was a beautiful dress, glowing with enchantment, and Pat's pink taffeta, which had seemed so appropriate for Valentine's Day, suddenly looked dowdy and juvenile.

"Oh, yes," Gwen said. "Clyde is divine. Look what he sent me!"

She opened the corsage box, which had been lying on the table, and lifted out a white orchid. Pat compressed her lips, trying to tell herself that orchids meant nothing to her. But the effort was useless, and she was racked with envy as she watched Gwen pinning hers on with smug satisfaction before the mirror.

The call came up for Gwen, "Clyde Warner for Gwen Gordon," and seizing a velvet wrap, she turned in the doorway and waved farewell to Pat.

"We'll see you at the dance," she said. "Tell your Tim we must be sure to trade dances."

She was gone, and Pat was alone with her misery. She sat down on the bed and held her head, wishing she had never come. Why was it, she wondered bitterly, that girls like Gwen could always think of things to say that she, Pat, could never find answers for? Why was it that Gwen could make her feel so like a child in five minutes of catty conversation?

If only Tim would get there, she thought passionately, if she could be with him, she would be all right. She finished dressing, put on her earrings, found her coat, which was not velvet nor formally dressy, and waited impatiently for the call.

15

The moment Pat saw the box in Tim's hand, as she came down the steps toward him, she thought of the orchid. She had forgotten about orchids while she waited, thinking only of how much she needed Tim. But now, seeing the box, a wave of triumph swept over her. Nothing would matter, not Gwen's insinuation, nor her inferior feeling about her dress, if Tim had chosen this moment to prove her value by giving her an orchid. She untied the string as he watched, trying not to seem overeager. Inside were two white gardenias.

"Oh, Tim!" Pat cried brightly, grateful that the words came easily before her throat choked up with disappointment: "It's beautiful! Thank you so much."

He looked pleased. "You said once you thought gardenias were so luxurious. I thought you'd like them tonight. And here is a tiny valentine. I don't know if you can wear it tonight, but I liked the idea."

In the second box he gave her was a pink-enamel heart-shaped pin, with a gold key dangling from it, and the words inscribed across it, "I give to you the key to my heart."

"Oh, I love it!" And she really meant it.

133

She pinned on her corsage and fastened the key to his heart upon it, comforted with the reflection that even if Tim didn't understand her feeling about orchids, he found charming ways of telling her he loved her. She glanced up and met his eyes, soft with happiness and shining like those of a child looking at a Christmas tree.

"You're beautiful tonight," he whispered, holding her coat for her. "Pink is my favorite color."

She took his arm, her confidence restored. And then to test her own reassurance she said: "I thought perhaps pink was childish when I saw Gwen's dress tonight. She's wearing red."

"I can't stand red!" Tim said immediately. "Your dress is perfect."

She laughed happily as she matched her step to his, and they walked slowly across campus to the gym.

On the dance floor, decorated with red hearts, suspended on long red streamers from the rafters, and flying cupids with bows and arrows, she was reminded of dances in the high school gym. They danced around the floor, traded dances with one or two of Tim's friends, avoided meeting Gwen, and chatted with lots of people. During one dance, Gwen passed close to them and waved, smiling too brightly.

"He gave her the most gorgeous orchid," Pat could not help saying. "Did you see it?"

Tim immediately craned his neck to see the orchid, now almost hidden by other couples.

"They're not worth the money," he said flatly. "Eight dollars for a corsage! Why, I'd be out of my head to spend that kind of money."

Pat was silent. Eight dollars was too much for Tim to

134

spend for flowers for a dance, and none knew it better than she. On the other hand, weren't there times when a symbol meant more than the dollars it cost? Tim would think bread was more important than roses, and Pat was sure that it was not. But then, she had never been hungry. She sighed over the complexity of the argument.

"Tired, sweety?" Tim looked down solicitously. "Want to sit down for a while?"

He found a couple of folding chairs, and Pat sank down on the hard narrow seat, grateful to be off her feet. One of the disillusionments of growing up had been the discovery that high heels were as uncomfortable as her parents had told her they would be. For months after she had gotten her first heels, she had countered this dictum with a sense of triumph, sure that she knew better. Now she wanted to slip her feet out of her shoes and didn't dare for fear she would not be able to get them on again.

She leaned back and watched the crowd swirl past, while Tim went away to fetch her a cup of punch and threaded his way precariously through the dancers to join her again.

Sipping the punch gratefully, she wondered why at her first college dance everything seemed so normal, so exactly like so many dances. It was Valentine's Day, the festival for sweethearts, and what was the difference? Except that she had the key to his heart! And even that did not mean as much as it should, Pat thought. She missed the elated excitement she had felt about Tim up until a couple of weeks ago. Let's face it, she thought. Now that she was used to being here at Tim's college dance, marriage was not as important as it had been last night when the visit seemed overwhelmingly new and different. She glanced at Tim, and he was watching the dance floor with a cheerful expression. He turned to her.

"Something wrong?" he asked. "You look kind of upset about something, Pat. What's the trouble?"

"Oh, nothing," she said. "Maybe I'm tired."

"Look," he said, "let's get out of here. Let's go out to the corridor or somewhere where we can talk."

"We can talk here," she said. But when Gwen danced past glancing at them alertly, Pat changed her mind. "All right," she got up, "you know this place better than I do."

They made their way out to the main lobby, a large marble-floored space, with flights of steps going up to the second floor on either side and deep-embrasured doors opening from the lobby into offices and locker rooms. Two other couples had already retired to secluded niches, but the space seemed enough unoccupied to give an illusion of privacy.

Pat followed Tim up the marble steps, wondering how many other dances he had attended when he had led his date to this spot. How many times had he sat up here with Gwen? She tried to discipline her thoughts, hating herself for being like this. They gained the top step and sat down facing each other.

"Did I tell you how much I like that dress?" Tim reached for Pat's hands. "You look gorgeous this weekend. It seems such a long time since I saw you at Christmas."

"I know," Pat murmured. "It bothers me, the way we're both changing while we're separated. What if we found we were entirely different people by the time I'm in college?"

He hugged her close and laid his head against hers.

136

"I worry about that all the time," he said soberly. "You're still in high school, and they say the big change comes in college. What if I should lose you?"

She looked at him quickly; his mouth was drawn in a tight line at the thought.

"*You* didn't change like that," she scoffed gently. "Why should I?"

"No, I didn't change that much," he said seriously. "But I was older to begin with. Sometimes I lie awake at night trying to figure out ways that we could get married sooner — maybe next summer. If we were changing together and growing together, it would be so much easier."

Pat listened with her head bent. Until this weekend, she had been the one who was impatient to get married. Now that Tim was concerned about cutting short the interval of waiting, she knew that she was no longer so anxious to hurry things as she had been last Christmas.

She was changing, as he had feared she would, and yet not as he feared, because her love for him had not changed. But now that she had found a personal goal, something truly important to her, she was a different person; she was someone who had a purpose to carry out, a purpose that must share her interest as well as Tim.

"Did I tell you what I want to do?" she asked abruptly.

He looked puzzled. "You've told me we want to get married." He sounded confidently teasing. "You haven't changed that, have you?"

"No," she shook her head. "I still want to get married. But now there's something else too. You remember I wrote you about the *Shrew?*" Her eyes looked dreamily into the spaces of the marble hall. "I want to do something with theater work. I don't know what it will be

137

yet — acting, directing, producing, maybe teaching — But I've decided to go to Northwestern next year. I want to go into the School of Speech."

She stopped, aware that Tim looked less enthusiastic than she felt about having found a college goal.

"That's fine," he said with an effort. "But you're not going to work very long, Pat. After all, you're going to be too busy with me to spend time in theater work after we're married."

"I won't be that busy," she said. "Look, honey, you'll be wrapped up in your work, and we can share each other's work. I may not have a full-time job, but there'll always be something to do."

"It's probably a good thing," he agreed, sounding as if he were being practical against his will. "Only it's so different from anything we've ever done together. I feel it might come between us."

"I wouldn't want that to happen." Pat hugged her knees and stared into the shadows. "But I feel as if this is something I have to do. I mean, if I gave it up now, when I've found out how important it is to me, some day it might really come between us."

He kissed her as if he were trying to reassure both of them.

"The trouble is we have to wait so long," he said again, "and everything changes in the waiting — you, me, the world."

"Better it should change now," said Pat, feeling old and wise, "than turn on us when it's too late. Oh, Tim, darling, don't be so afraid of life! I feel the same about you as I always did, but I feel different now about me. Life gets more interesting all the time, and I'm not in such a hurry

138

any more to get married. Now there is more reason to wait and more to do with our time while we are waiting."

"Of course you're right," he conceded, "only in some ways it was more exciting last summer."

Pat smiled at him comfortingly. "In some ways we've already begun to grow up," she said, "even when I don't want to I find myself understanding what my parents are talking about. And when we do get married" — her eyes were dreamy as she thought of the future — "we'll be ready for it."

Tim said nothing, squeezing her hand tightly as if he wanted to hold on to her, and the scent of the gardenia corsage floated up to her. It was a delicious scent: sweet and penetrating and rich in the memory of their first dance date together.

The scent of gardenias would always remind her, Pat knew in swift prevision, of the night she began to grow up.

16

The realization that Tim was not interested in the theater had passed across Pat's mind almost unnoticed in the emotion of the Valentine dance weekend. But alone on the train Sunday afternoon, watching the scene of the campus weekend disappear with nostalgic regret for the shortness of time, Pat turned her thoughts toward next Saturday night when the first of the Northwestern Theater plays was scheduled, and regret dried up and blew away in the uprush of anticipation.

She should feel more dismal about leaving Tim, she thought. But she told herself it was only reasonable to fill her time with other activities and occupy her mind with other thoughts than Tim's absence while they were apart. And then she remembered the conversation during the dance, and a wave of alarm trembled across her mind.

For the first time there was a strong difference in their interests. Her mother had remarked several times that they had nothing in common, but Pat had always told her with lighthearted assurance that they had each other. Now she realized that there had been nothing she really cared about doing without Tim until she had discovered the theater. It was ironic that, when she found the goal she had been looking for only halfheartedly, it must be something Tim had no interest in at all.

He'll have to get used to the fact that this means a great deal to me, she thought. He'll have to learn to like some things, even if he never did before. And she believed that he couldn't help it if he once experienced the excitement that she had found. She began making plans for spring vacation, when he would be home for almost ten days. Only six more weeks until he would be home again. Those six weeks went unbelievably fast. When Pat said to her mother in astonishment that it didn't seem possible that time could really fly like that, Mrs. Marlowe reminded her that she had never been wrapped up in a creative interest before.

Mrs. Marlowe had been interested in dramatics and had pursued a highly successful career in " little theater " work until she had married and found that she wanted to write. Now, instead of feeling overshadowed by her mother's achievements as she had felt so often last year, Pat was pleased that her mother's background gave her so much authority and knowledge, and they had frequent discussions, which Pat found stimulating and illuminating.

Her mother enjoyed watching the important dramatic programs on television. She had opinions about the long-time stars as well as the new stars that Pat felt were surprisingly perceptive for one who had been away from theater work for so long. Unconsciously her opinion of her mother's experience went up, and she found herself considering her mother's ideas more attentively than before.

When Mrs. Marlowe said, " You cannot be sure at this age what you are going to want all the rest of your life,"

Pat agreed noncommittally. But she thought about her mother's words very seriously. Once she would have cried in quick rejection, " Oh, yes I can." Now she reflected that her mother had been right very often in the past year and perhaps she was going to be right again.

At any rate, Pat was willing to slow down and proceed with caution when her mother suggested that she might be committing herself to a program that seemed dubious. She could look at her secret hope of being a Broadway star someday with realism and humor, and tell herself it could be fun if the lightning happened to strike her. But otherwise she could have a wonderful time teaching school — as long as she was teaching dramatics.

Jack Willis took her to the first of the University Theater productions the Saturday after her return from Crandall. Pat had been uneasy about dating him after the cast party. But he sounded cheerful and insouciant, he had been carelessly attentive in school, and she persuaded herself that he had been suffering only from an unforeseen mood, probably a letdown following the *Shrew* production, and it didn't mean a thing.

This impression was reinforced on Saturday night's date. Jack was gay and humorous. He was seriously interested in the play itself, which was an extremely fast-moving, expertly finished interpretation of Molière's *Mischief-maker*, and they had a wonderful time talking about the play: forecasting successful professional futures for the leads, comparing production techniques with their own experience at high school, talking about what each of them might be doing in some future day in theater work.

When she left Jack that night, Pat felt as if she had had a stimulating experience that left her satisfied and exhilarated. It was wonderful to be able to talk like that! She thought of Tim with a pang. That response and interest on his part was the only thing missing in their relationship.

The next two plays came at fortnightly intervals, and she went with Jack both times, looking forward to each date, confident that they had struck an understanding that filled a need for both of them without getting confused with romance. The third time they went to the Northwestern Theater, the conversation seemed to be overcast with the kind of sentimental yearning Pat had noticed the night of the cast party. She was aware of it during intermission and instinctively recoiled. During the last act she could hardly keep her mind on the play, trying to figure out why she felt like this about Jack. They had spent so many hours talking about each other's problems that she had felt he was a sympathetic audience. And yet when he made a demand for attention, as he had the night of the cast party and again tonight, her dislike surprised her because it seemed unreasonable.

When they talked over the play on the way home, the satisfaction that had been so warm on the last two dates was missing. She kept trying to fight down a strong feeling that she didn't care tonight what Jack thought about the play, and even a compulsion to disagree with him on points where she felt no disagreement, just to be contrary.

At her door he kissed her good night. The kiss was unexpected, because she was not aware that they were through talking.

"Don't," she said, turning her head sharply.

"Pat," he pleaded, "you don't know how I feel about you. I'm crazy about you, honey. And we like the same things; we've got the same interests — "

She pulled away. "Jack, I'm sorry. I hate to make any-one feel bad. And I've had a good time going to these plays with you. But I don't feel like being romantic with you. I'm sorry, but that's how it is."

"What does it take?"

She shook her head. "I don't know. All I know is that I feel that way about Tim and I never seem to about anyone else. Tim's the one, and there's no use arguing about it."

It proved something, she told her mother the next day. It proved that love needed something more than a common interest.

"I feel so sorry for Jack," Pat said, and she did feel sorry when she was away from him. "It must be depressing to fall for two girls, one right after another, and not under-stand why they don't fall for you. I feel the way Nan did — what's the use of keeping it going, when you know it won't work?"

But even as she recognized that a common interest was not enough, she still faced the problem of fitting her new goal into her life with Tim.

"You can't build all your life around Tim's preferences," her mother said, "even though you think now that he will always be the center of it. You should develop some kind of independent personality, and so should he."

"He isn't going to like the kind of plays I like to go to," Pat brooded. "He doesn't like anything but musical comedies, and I've already gotten tired of them. He can't stand Shakespeare, and I love it, since the *Shrew*."

"He ought to learn to enjoy something he didn't under-stand before," said Mrs. Marlowe incisively. "He won't be a very interesting person ten years from now if he stops growing at this time."

Even as she rushed to Tim's defense, Pat could not ignore her mother's suggestion.

"If he grows in intellectual interest," her mother observed, "and if you continue to, somewhere along the line you will find something you both can enjoy."

"I'd like to take him to that Shakespeare play the last Saturday of his vacation," Pat said wistfully. "I'd like to *make* him like it. Anyway, he'd feel so upset if I went without him, I don't see how I can do that, and I simply can't miss it."

"Could you turn in your own ticket and get two together?"

"I'll see what I can do."

The last play was *Richard the Third*, and Pat felt after seeing the Olivier production on TV that it was the most important play of the series. Jack would not be there; he was driving to Florida as he had planned last Christmas. But feeling as she did about him she could not bring herself to ask him for his ticket in order to take Tim.

On the last day of school Marge Wilder, who had been going to every play, mentioned that she was leaving for Florida with her parents that night.

"How wonderful!" Pat said enthusiastically, with a dim idea that if so many of her friends went to Florida, she herself might soon be going there. And then she remembered Marge's ticket and changed her tone to shocked dismay. "Oh, Marge, that means you'll miss the play on Saturday."

"I know, and it makes me sick," said Marge. "The folks made these reservations before I even got the tickets, so naturally they can't change them now, and even for *Richard the Third* I'm not going to miss Florida."

"May I buy your ticket?"

"Of course! I'm glad you mentioned it."

"Tim is going to be home that week, and I've been trying to figure out how I could see that play without making him mad about Saturday night. This will solve the whole problem."

Marge laughed and handed her the ticket from her purse. "I hope he likes it."

"He'd better like it," said Pat. "I've been waiting all spring for this one."

She was sure that he would when she went down to meet Tim's train by Saturday morning. Remembering the *Shrew*, she believed that anyone, even Tim, could get enthusiastic about Shakespeare.

Tim swung down from the train, glowing with anticipation.

I thought today would never get here," he said when he had kissed her. "Time sure dragged after you went home from the dance."

"I thought Gwen would be keeping you busy," Pat teased him.

Tim cocked an eye at her and made an expression of distaste.

"Not that girl," he said. "After you had been up there, it wasn't the same. She understood how things were with you and me, and after you left she concentrated on Clyde more than ever. She wouldn't even give me the time of day. I've been lonesome."

"We've got a week to make up for it." Pat spoke a little absently, concentrating on her driving as she made her way into the traffic stream.

"I sent in an application for transfer to Northwestern

146

next year," Tim said unexpectedly. "They've got some courses I want that Crandall doesn't have, and one year away is enough."

Pat said nothing, intent on the road and the streams of traffic whizzing by. But his words struck her with stunning impact. It would be heavenly to have Tim around all the time.

Or would it?

"We could study together; we could eat lunch together," he said, planning ahead.

"I'll be in the School of Speech," she reminded him. "I don't know what my program will be like, except that there'll be lots of play rehearsal after class hours."

"That's O.K.," he said generously. "I'll even go to see every play you're in."

"They're wonderful plays," Pat said, almost forgetting the road in her enthusiasm as she turned to glance at Tim. He seized the wheel and straightened out the car. "Eyes on the road, honey!" She focused on the road again, but her mind now was on plays.

"We're going to see one of the University Theater productions next Saturday."

"We are?"

"I wrote you about the series I had tickets for, remember?"

"Sure, but I didn't know you had to go during vacation."

"This isn't vacation at the university."

"What's the play?"

"*Richard the Third.*"

"Shakespeare?"

"Yes."

Pat was aware of a depressing lack of enthusiasm in

Tim's question and she was irritated. She tried to be understanding.

"If you don't want to go to it, darling, I'll go without you. I don't want to drag you around to places you don't like."

"But the last night of my vacation!" He sounded outraged. "Why not just skip it and go to a good movie?"

They were approaching a zone of merging traffic, and Pat had good reason not to talk. So she said nothing for about half a mile, while Tim, tense as always with any other driver than himself, sat rigidly beside her, his eyes on the traffic too.

"Anyway the whole decision is a week away," she said comfortingly. "Don't worry about it. What would you like to do tonight?"

Tim's plans for vacation were to spend all the time he could with Pat. He was anxious to see her brother and parents, of whom he was very fond, and it did not make much difference what they did in the evening as long as they were together.

"We could go out to lunch somewhere," he said, leaning on the door of the car a moment, in front of his own house. "If Connie is around, we might see her this afternoon. Tonight let's go dancing."

"It all sounds wonderful," said Pat.

And so it did. There was nothing she would rather do just then than fool around visiting with friends all day and dancing all night.

The question of what would happen, when there was something she would rather do than spend all her time with Tim, raised its ugly head, and she ignored it, confident that it could be answered when it had to be.

17

They did all the things that Tim had planned. The dance on Saturday night was delightful: the music was good, the setting was glamorous, they saw many of Pat's high school friends there, and it was romantic to be together again. On Sunday they went to church together and dined with the Davises. This custom gave Pat a comfortable sense of stability and permanence. In the afternoon they went for a ride and saw the young leaves feathering out, the daffodils starring lawns and edging driveways, the first brilliant hyacinths, the early scarlet tulips.

" Spring really is the most exciting season," Pat said, her eyes soft with looking at the loveliness around them.

" It is," Tim agreed. He kissed her to celebrate spring.

They ate supper with the Marlowes, and Tim told Denny all about Crandall athletics, and how he had played basketball during the winter and might go out for track in the spring. He listened to Denny talk about plans for Little League baseball. They watched television.

" Tomorrow night there is going to be a tremendous production," Pat announced, studying the program during the commercial. " Tim, I want you to see this with me. Maurice Evans is going to star in Shaw's *Caesar and Cleopatra.*

Isn't that terrific? I saw him in *The Taming of the Shrew* a few weeks ago, and he is simply great."

"Do we hafta look at *Caesar and Cleopatra?*" Denny demanded, in quick grievance. "That's the time Sherlock Holmes comes on."

Pat appealed to her mother. "He can see Sherlock any week," she argued, "and this is a special performance. It won't happen again for years."

"I think in a case like this Pat should see her choice," Mrs. Marlowe ruled. Denny subsided, sulking, until the comedian returned to the screen and diverted him from his wrongs. Pat held Tim's hand and murmured: "I can't wait for that performance tomorrow night. I know you'll like it." Tim said nothing.

On Monday, Pat slept till noon, and Tim came over for lunch. In the afternoon they went shopping. Pat wanted a new hat, which Tim declared she didn't need, and he needed some socks, which he bought in five minutes. The hat took an hour and a half, and the hunt included four stores. Even Tim did not mind, since they were together. They separated reluctantly for dinner, with Tim's promise to return at seven thirty to be on time for the television show.

At eight o'clock Denny departed scowling darkly to read a library book. Mike went over to see Connie, declaring that G. B. Shaw was too deep for him, Mr. Marlowe went out to a meeting, and Pat and Tim watched *Caesar and Cleopatra* with Mrs. Marlowe.

Pat leaned forward in her chair, studying every detail of production, forgetting all about Tim in her absorption. The sets were original and interesting; she was enchanted with Evans' interpretation and inflection. She thought

150

Cleopatra was overdone, but the play was stimulating and amusing.

"Too talky," Tim commented at the end of the second act.

She glanced at him as if he were an unwarranted interruption.

"If you don't like it, we'll shut it off," she said with a martyred inflection.

"No, no," Tim sounded alarmed at the idea of offending her. "I want to see the end of it. Don't shut off on my account."

"I like it," said Mrs. Marlowe.

They sat back to watch the third act, but some of the enchantment was gone for Pat, and her thoughts were divided between the play on the screen and background protests in her mind against Tim's evident lack of interest. When it was over, she rose.

"I loved it," she said flatly, as if someone might contradict her. "I'm sorry if you were bored, Tim, but I like that kind of play."

"I wasn't bored," Tim protested indignantly. "Not all the time anyway. I thought there were some parts where he talked too much. Besides, I thought he was supposed to fall in love with the girl."

"He did!" Pat cried, indignant at his lack of perception. "Couldn't you understand that part of it? But he was too old for her."

"I'll say he was," Tim grinned, as if a joke might ease the tension.

"I thought it was a very interesting production," Mrs. Marlowe remarked. "I remember the first time I saw it, about thirty years ago. This was better."

151

Pat said no more. She was glad her mother had liked it, but deeply disturbed that she and Tim felt so differently about something that was so important to her. Saturday's play was taking on the aspects of a test case.

They went to a movie Tuesday night; they looked at television again on Wednesday night; and both days they spent the afternoons together. By Thursday afternoon when Tim appeared there was nothing left for them to do or talk about.

Pat prepared a tea tray and carried it into the living room where her mother was sitting.

"That looks delightful," Mrs. Marlowe said. "Thank you very much, Pat." She was reading a heavy volume called *Black Lamb and Grey Falcon* and she poured herself a cup of tea and prepared to go back to her reading.

"Mother, we've got a problem." Pat gestured to Tim to sit down and poured tea for them.

Mrs. Marlowe looked up, marked her page, and closed her book.

"What seems to be the trouble?"

"There's nothing to do."

Mrs. Marlowe's mouth seemed to catch in an uncontrollable little smile.

"You sound exactly like Denny. My goodness, a couple of healthy young adults on vacation ought to be able to find plenty to do! Why don't you go bowling?"

"The alleys are closed on Thursday, and anyway that's too expensive. Tim hasn't got any money."

"How about —" Mrs. Marlowe stopped and frowned, evidently finding her own difficulty in thinking of ideas. "How about something in Chicago, like a museum?" she turned to Tim.

He shook his head, frowning distastefully. " I hate museums," he said. " I saw all I wanted to of them when I was a kid."

"Anyway, it's too late for this afternoon," Pat said. " We're trying to find something for tonight."

" How about bridge? "

" No partners. Connie and Mike are busy, and everybody else is out of town. Do you and Daddy want to play bridge with us? "

" Daddy has a meeting and he doesn't like bridge anyway. You know I can never get him to play cards."

" What did you do when you were young? " Pat wondered. " There doesn't seem to be anything happening around here."

" Well, for one thing," Mrs. Marlowe sat up straight and looked at both of them, " we couldn't spend every day together, all day long, the way you kids do. Daddy was working and he lived farther away, and I saw him twice a week all the time we were engaged."

" How hideous," Pat observed.

Tim said, " But we want to be together all the time, and there's no reason why we shouldn't be, because we're both free and we have lots of time." He smiled engagingly as if he were sure she would understand.

" No reason," said Mrs. Marlowe, " except that you will wear out more quickly. For instance, what about today? You're bored and have nothing to do because you've been together so steadily this week that you've done everything too soon."

Tim shook his head, looking at once unconvinced and baffled by the situation.

" When we're married, it will be different," he said.

"It's this time in between while we're waiting that gets dull."

"But you've got years to go through before you can get married," Mrs. Marlowe said. "You can't afford to be bored for two or three years or you won't even want to marry each other."

Pat set down her teacup.

"Oh, well, we'll think of something. We can always go to a movie."

They ended up going to a movie that evening, but it was a singularly uninspired Western, which Tim claimed he liked and which Pat found stupid.

The whole trouble was, she recognized, tossing restlessly that night before she could go to sleep, that they were suspended in this void of time where waiting seemed endless.

When she was in school, there were exciting things to do, and away from Tim she could see a clear pattern of preparation for the future. But when she was with Tim, as she had been this week, they kept dwelling upon a plan for marriage about which nothing could be done, no matter how much they discussed it.

They spent one morning looking at china, and Tim had no preference.

"Anything you like is all right, dear," he said, as they examined one unfamiliar pattern after another. Pat, with little preference herself, felt that he ought to have some ideas. He ought to help her choose; he ought to say, "Yes, this is it," and "No, not that one."

Instead, he looked at everything with the expression of a stranger in a foreign land and waved his hand and said, "As long as it isn't too expensive." Pat, wanting to take some definite step that would make their marriage seem more sure and more immediate, could not bring herself to buy even a cup and saucer, recognizing that facing the eternal enemy, Time, she might change her mind several times about china.

They looked at silver, and Tim's reaction there was contrary both to Pat's preferences and to his feeling about china. He liked three or four patterns that she did not, and he did not like anything that she did. At the end of vacation week they were no closer to a pattern than they had been before.

"I wouldn't try to hurry a decision," said Mrs. Marlowe, when Pat consulted her about the problem. "There is no rush."

That was the whole trouble, Pat raged silently, feeling as if the enemy were taking cloudy multiple forms and ringing her love in irresistible hostility. It was going to be paralyzed with inaction if something didn't happen. When she was with Tim, time stood still, and although that was the romantic dream of the poets, for them the effect was different. She could hardly wait for next week, when school would start again, wheels would begin rolling, and time would pass, quickly, quickly.

By Saturday night she was torn between her anticipation for the University Theater play and her fear that it might open the rift between herself and Tim that she had been sensing all week, although she believed that he did not suspect it.

She tried to prepare him for the play by talking about the other version of *Richard the Third* that she had seen, describing the excitement she had felt, letting him know how important this event was for her. Although Tim, with

155

loving regard for her enthusiasm, refrained from any dampening comments, still there was a lack of response and an obvious disinterest that left Pat feeling alone in spite of love.

She could not help remembering how eagerly Jack Willis discussed every aspect of the theater, how often he called to her attention something she had overlooked, how interested he was in her reactions, and how vividly they discussed their differences of opinion on a performance. Jack and she had this lively common interest, and yet they had nothing more. She almost wished on Saturday night that Tim were not going with her.

When they arrived, Bob Kent, Ron Flower, and Willa were there.

"Hi, kids!" Pat forgot her fears for the evening in her joy at seeing this group again. "You've all met Tim Davis, haven't you? Tim, you met Ron and Willa at the cast party last fall. And Bob Kent."

They acknowledged each other cordially, and Pat sat between Tim and Bob, who pointed out some program notes of special interest. Pat remembered some of the actors from a previous performance, and discussed them with him. As the lights went down she glanced at Tim. He was looking as if he had come alone, his program lying disregarded on his lap, his eyes fixed on some distant focus beyond the curtained stage. Pat reached over and patted his hand.

She felt very tender toward him at the moment, thinking about the effort he was making for her sake, and convinced that he would be rewarded with the same light of understanding that had illuminated her own life this past winter.

The curtain went up and Richard strode to the footlights and pronounced in tones of doom,

"Now is the winter of our discontent

Made glorious summer by this sun of York,"
and the play was begun.

Pat listened to the rolling lines with growing absorption. This Northwestern student was doing as well, it seemed to her, as Olivier had done, at least in the opening scene. Then she began to see differences of interpretation and she became engrossed in trying to decide whether or not she liked this interpretation better than the one she had seen on TV. She turned to Bob to consult with him between scenes, and he thought he liked the Olivier version better.

Pat thought not. This was the classical production done in the seventeenth-century style in which it had first been performed, with almost no scenery to distract the eye from the actors, and it had great power.

By the end of the third act she realized that Tim was shifting restlessly in his seat and she turned to him.

"Isn't this tremendous?" she begged. "Don't you love it? I didn't realize it could be so good."

"Yeah, it's O. K.," he said. "Very good — I guess. How much longer is it?"

"There are five acts and no intermission," Pat said incisively.

Tim groaned. Then he grinned at her. "I can stand it if you can, I guess."

She made no answer and inside she felt cold. She did not turn to Bob again but she concentrated on the play, feeling, as it went on in growing intensity, more and more alone.

When the play was over, Tim jumped up, glad to be out of the seat where he had been sitting so long, and helped her into the aisle. The spell of the play lingered, and Pat walked up the aisle dreaming of dark Richard with the music of Shakespeare's lines sounding behind his image. Carefully she folded the program and tucked it away for safekeeping.

"Want some coffee or ice cream or something?" Tim asked. "We could go over to the Kampus Kitchen."

"Let's." Pat wondered if Tim recognized this conflict, which she felt was basic.

They found a small booth at the Kampus Kitchen, and both ordered coffee and sweet rolls. While they waited for their order, Bob and Ron and Willa came in and sat down across the aisle from them two booths ahead. Pat could see them clearly from where she sat, and she realized that they were talking with animated enjoyment about the play. Unhappiness pierced her like a knife: she could not talk to Tim like that. They could not share her special interest on any ground at all. She wondered if she could face this division all her life.

"What's the matter, sweetheart?" Tim was solicitous. "You look as if something was bothering you."

The waitress set down the sweet rolls and coffee before them and withdrew. Pat broke her roll and buttered a small piece.

"Something is bothering me," she said. "And I think it's serious. It's this business of plays and the theater. It means so much to me, and you don't like any of the things I like at all."

Tim stirred his coffee, his face very thoughtful.

"I know," he said at last. "I don't seem to like the

heavy stuff. Shakespeare! Now the play was very good tonight. I could see lots of things about it that were good. But I couldn't say I really enjoyed it, like a good musical, for instance."

He smiled at her as if he hoped to divert her from her argument.

"I'm beginning to hate musicals," Pat said intensely. "That's the whole trouble. You like something so different from what I like. Oh, Tim, what are we going to do about it?"

He slumped back in the booth, watching the circles his spoon was making in his coffee cup.

"Do we have to do something about it? I mean, why can't you go to the plays you like and enjoy them without me? We've got lots of other things we can enjoy together."

"But it would mean so much more if you like my plays too," Pat said.

Tim sat up and leaned forward. "I know, darling. And it would mean a lot to me if you liked jazz music. But I don't see that that's too important."

"But when we're married — if we get married — " Tim shot her a quick dark glance, and Pat went on, "I'm probably going to want to spend time with 'little theater' groups or acting in plays besides going to them, and it will separate us a lot."

"I'll go to everything you're in," he promised, again trying to sound a light note. "Honestly, darling, it isn't as important as you're making it."

"But I don't want to be doing all those things alone," Pat cried. "I want you doing things with me. That's the whole point of being in love; it's the whole point of being married."

159

He leaned forward again, as serious as she was. "What can we do about it?"

"You could make an effort," she said. "You could try to like serious plays."

"I do try," he said. "I tried last Monday for that TV play. I tried tonight."

He had tried, she knew, and with a sensation of defeat she recognized that it wasn't good enough. She rubbed her forehead as if it would help her to think.

"I don't know what we can do," she murmured. "Only perhaps we shouldn't plan to get married as soon as we thought we could. I'll have to figure this out."

Tim had no answer. They were both silent all the way back to Allandale, each grappling with his own thoughts. When Tim said good night, he crushed her to him.

"You can't let something like this come between us," he muttered fiercely. "I love you too much. And you love me, Pat; you know you do."

Shaken, Pat nodded. "I do love you, Tim. But we'll have to see how this is going to work out."

Alone in her bedroom afterward, she wondered how they could work it out. And if not — how could she ever break with Tim?"

18

When did you say Joanne's baby is due?" Mrs. Marlowe asked Pat the second week in April.

Pat, reading her letter from Tim, replied almost without hearing the question, "The eighth," and then as her own words rang an alarm bell she jerked her head up and asked: "Why? Is it here?"

"No. I haven't heard a thing about it," Mrs. Marlowe said. "Today's the eleventh. Lots of times babies are late. I was just interested."

"I'll ask Connie about it tonight."

She had almost forgotten about Joanne's baby in the complications of vacation week and the attendant excitement of returning to school. Nan was back from Florida, bronzed and full of chatter about what a marvelous time she had had, what a heavenly place they had stayed in, and what wonderful people she had met — crowds of college men. The announcement of tryouts for the final play of the year was posted. It would be *Arsenic and Old Lace*, and Pat wanted to be in it, the last play she would work in at high school.

She folded Tim's letter, tucked it into her notebook and went upstairs to study before supper, forgetting about

Joanne again as she thought deeply about her problem with Tim.

He was coming home more often this spring, he wrote. And she ought to be delighted, ecstatic, completely happy about seeing him frequently. Instead she felt this uneasy, guilty reaction that his coming home was going to interfere with lots of things she wanted to do. He wasn't going to enjoy himself the weekend the play was produced, and that would leave her feeling responsible. She sighed heavily and reread his letter again: "It might be better to go ahead and plan to get married next year. When we are married, we won't have these differences."

She felt trapped, and her mind thrashed about wildly trying to find someone to blame. Her mother should have stopped her, she thought. But that was no comfort. Pat could remember as if it were yesterday the questions her mother had tried to make her consider, the advice, rejected over and over again, about not being in too much of a hurry, the times her mother had said she did not see what Pat and Tim had in common, the assurances that she would feel differently as she grew older. And Pat had believed, as violently as she believed she loved Tim, that parents never understood their children, that they didn't trust them to have any sense or to use it.

She sat down in the small antique rocker and stared out of the window, thinking hard, harder than she had ever thought before in her life. She had chosen to marry Tim, determined to marry him as soon as she finished high school. And now she knew with a sense of self-betrayal that she did not want to marry him right away.

She separated that thought from the others and examined it. She still loved him. But she didn't want to be rushed into marriage next summer, and she wanted to talk it over with someone. Not her mother! Something deep within her recoiled from that. Even though her mother would never say so in so many words, there would be between them the sense of " I told you so," and " I knew it all the time."

Not Connie! She was too young and she did not understand even as much as Mrs. Marlowe.

Joanne! She was the only one Pat could think of who could know about these problems.

That reminded Pat again of Joanne's baby, and she sprang to the telephone with real urgency. Suppose Joanne was already in the hospital and couldn't talk to her?

The phone rang three times, four, five, and Pat let it ring once more.

" Hello? "

" Joanne? This is Pat. I'm so glad I caught you."

" Well, I'm not! " Joanne sounded as if she were laughing. " I'm supposed to be in the hospital by now."

" Oh, of course, I hope you don't have to wait much longer."

" I'm used to waiting by now. Seems as if there's always something to wait for, and I might as well be philosophical about it."

Pat laughed, cheered already. " Could I come over and talk to you tonight? I've got a problem and I think you're the one who might have some answers."

" Fine," Joanne said promptly. " Connie is going to the library tonight. She wants to get an early start on a term paper. So we'll have a private conference. Why don't you come over around seven fifteen? "

" I'll be there," said Pat. " Thanks so much. You're sure

163

this isn't interrupting anything?"

"Not a thing except a couple of empty hours that I'm glad to interrupt. You come along."

Joanne was wonderful, Pat thought for the fifteenth time, as she hung up the telephone.

"Mom?" she went downstairs to set the table for supper. "Joanne is still home. She doesn't know how long it will be. I'm going over to see her about seven fifteen for a little while."

She was late in spite of her eagerness. As she was about to leave the house Jack Willis called. She hadn't heard from him for days, and as he sometimes did, he talked on and on about his week in Florida and some plays he had seen on TV. Pat noticed with annoyance that he never said, "Is this a good time to talk?" No, he assumed that she'd be free and happy to listen, because her part of the call was almost all listening. She finally managed to break in and say: "Jack, I've got to go now. I've got an appointment, but thanks for calling." As he hung up she knew he was annoyed.

"Men!" she muttered, as she rushed out the door.

Joanne looked prettier than ever, Pat thought. There was an expression of serenity and confidence in her eyes, happiness in her smile. She was sitting on a straight chair, which she laughed about, and finishing the dress she had been knitting.

"Me," she said, "the original lounger, condemned to sit up straight for nobody knows how long."

"But don't you hate this delay?"

Joanne shrugged. "It's tedious, but goodness, do you waste energy hating a thundershower at the wrong time? I learned when Jerry went off to sea that there's no use

164

wasting steam on a fact of life like the Navy or the weather or waiting for the baby. I've been waiting nine months now. A few more days won't matter a hundred years from now. But tell me about your problem. Connie has told me a lot about Tim, and he sounds like a darling. And I liked him when you brought him over."

"He is a darling," Pat said, feeling lonesome as she said the words. "I love him as much as ever. But something has happened to me. It isn't enough, the way things are now."

Joanne's eyes were bright with interest. She nodded. "I know exactly how you feel. When you're married, there are so many things to plan for and dream about and work toward. But when you're in school, love isn't enough to keep you going indefinitely. It wears out if you rely on it too much."

Pat nodded, already comforted at the thought of being so clearly understood.

"That's the way it is," she said, "and I don't know what to do about it. I still love Tim, and if anything broke us up for keeps, I think I'd die. I can't take a chance on losing him and then I wonder, if I married him too soon, would I lose him anyway? Would we spoil things seeing even more of each other than we do now?"

Joanne looked very thoughtful. "You mean, if you don't go ahead and get married, you might break up?"

"That's what worries me. I've been in some plays at school and now I'm crazy about the theater, but Tim doesn't like the kind of thing I like at all. He doesn't want to talk about actors and acting and he doesn't like Shakespeare *at all*. I feel so alone when we're together. I don't want something like this to come between Tim and me —

but what is going to happen in all those years later on? "

Joanne looked serious and she knitted several stitches with concentrated attention as if she were counting. Pat waited.

" You know, of course," Joanne said, as if she were speaking to another adult, and Pat listened gratefully, " you will probably be discovering new interests all the rest of your life. Your interest in dramatics is only the first thing, and each new thing will make your life richer." She looked up at Pat then. " I never looked at paintings till after I was married. Then I realized I wanted to hang something on the walls, and all of a sudden I was fascinated with paintings. I spent a lot of time at the art museums. I began reading about art and artists. Jerry never did see the point. It would have been more fun if he'd liked them the way I did " — she shrugged philosophically — " but it was nothing to separate us. Jerry got excited about the sea and exploration, somewhere along the line, and he kept dragging home books about Columbus and navigation and early sailing ships." Joanne laughed. " I hate the sea," she said with great cheerfulness, " but if Jerry likes it, that's fine with me. He's the one that's out there now."

" But didn't you feel kind of alone some way? " Pat demanded. " I mean, down inside? "

Joanne looked at her again with that clear understanding.

" The first few weeks we were married I felt as if we ought to do and like and think the same thing about everything," she confessed. " But when Jerry's orders came through and separated us, regardless of our feelings, I had time to figure things out alone at home. No matter how much you're in love, you've got an independent

166

personality to develop, and so has Tim. If you lean on each other too much, you can wear out your love and come to the point where you want to be alone for a while. Love Tim and let him love you, but don't feel that you are handicapped without his being in step with you all the way."

"I suppose so," Pat said, not sure that she agreed. "But how can you tell when it isn't a basic incompatibility?"

Joanne laughed and then cut it short. "I didn't mean to laugh at your question, because it's very important. You'll test the business of compatible temperaments in the time you are waiting — evidently you are thoroughly congenial in everything except this one special interest."

Pat nodded. "Nothing ever came between us before — and Tim doesn't think it's that important even now."

"Isn't there something Tim likes to do that you'd rather stay out of?"

Pat thought back. For so long now they had devoted every possible moment to being in each other's company that she found it hard to remember what Tim did before they began going steady.

"He's a high-fidelity fan," she recalled. "He's always working on his set and switching components and listening for flaws —" She wrinkled her nose in distaste, and Joanne laughed at her. "I like to listen to a good recording," Pat went on, "but I'm so bored with listening for twenty-thousand kilocycles and having Tim say, 'Hear that triangle?' and then switch onto jazz and talk about how deep the drum beat is!"

"There's your answer," said Joanne. "You and he ought to be able to spend some time apart, with other people, when each of you has a special interest like that. And another thing" — she glanced at Pat and then fixed her attention on casting off her knitting — "there are so many things to do with this time of your life. If you pass them by now you never get the same chance again. I think you ought to go out with other boys part of the time."

"I've been going out with Jack Willis," said Pat. "He feels the way I do about dramatics, but otherwise I don't like him."

"A common interest isn't the only thing," Joanne agreed. "You might find a great actor, who wanted to think of nothing but his profession and talk about it all the time, and he might have all sorts of drawbacks in other directions, like being selfish and demanding and hard to live with and maybe no good at supporting a family. You have to look for more than an interest in a husband."

Pat smiled radiantly. "I'm beginning to feel better since I've talked to you. For a while the conflict seemed impossible."

Joanne smiled back. "I've met Tim, and somehow I don't think it will be a mistake a year or two from now if you decide that he's still the one. But you're right when you think there is no hurry. If it's love, it will keep — if you give it a chance."

Pat got up, remembering her homework, and turned toward the door.

"It's been a big help to talk to you, Joanne. I think I know how to answer Tim's letter now. And I have a feeling everything will work out all right."

"Good luck!" Joanne was smiling again, and it seemed as if there was a radiance around her head as she stood in the open doorway.

"Good luck to *you*," Pat called.

19

The telephone rang at six the next morning, and Pat woke out of a sound sleep wondering what on earth — ! She stumbled sleepily to the telephone, sat down on the chair beside the table, and leaned her head against the wall.

"Pat?" It was Connie. "Joanne had a baby boy about two hours ago. Can you imagine? I'm an aunt!"

Pat was wide awake, although her eyes kept closing.

"Connie! I'm so glad! How big is he? How is Joanne? What is she going to call him? Two hours ago? Why, I was over there last night, and she had no idea —"

"She had to rush off at midnight, and we all went with her. I've been up all night and I'm not going to try to go to school today. They're going to call him Peter Foster, after Dad, and he's the cutest thing you ever saw. Eight and a half pounds and twenty-two inches long."

"Isn't that awfully tiny?"

The laughter of a proud and indulgent aunt bubbled over the wire.

"He's very long, they tell me. The doctor said this little guy is going to be big someday. And Joanne feels wonderful. She saw her baby, and everything is fine. I'm dead — I'm going to bed right now. But will you bring my assignments? I tried not to wake you too early, but I couldn't wait another minute."

Her mother was standing beside Pat, wrapped in a flowered quilted robe.

"Was that about Joanne?"

Pat gave her the news. "Don't let me forget Connie's books," she said, yawning deeply. "I'm going back to bed. I don't have to get up for another hour."

"I'm glad the news is good," said Mrs. Marlowe. "Time is certainly going by in a hurry. Imagine Joanne having a baby — Why, it seems like yesterday that she was hitting Mike with a shovel out in the sandbox when he wouldn't give her something she wanted!"

Pat went back to bed, smiling at her mother's reminiscence. It seemed to her, the way she used to hear it, that it was Mike who hit Joanne, and Joanne was at least three years older than Mike. It didn't seem so long ago, at that.

By now she was thoroughly awakened and in no mood to sleep again after all. She thought about Joanne and her son. At this time of the morning a baby seemed the most important thing in the world. And Tim would be wonderful with children. Look how nice he was with Denny, playing ping-pong with him, or tossing a football, or looking at whatever Denny wanted him to look at. It seemed, in spite of last night's conversation, important to have a family soon.

At six thirty she was too restless to stay in bed any longer, and she dressed and went down and made breakfast for her family. When she had her own house, she thought, as she measured out the coffee, she was not going to have any beat-up old aluminum cups around, like that one her mother kept for measuring soap. She was going to have glass ones. She was in the mood to live a new life as soon as possible. Discussing her problems with Joanne last night seemed to have solved them completely.

Denny came down.

"You here already?" he sounded suspicious. "How come?"

Pat was feeling motherly toward Denny, projecting Joanne's newborn son against the long perspective of growing up and seeing him at eleven.

"Joanne had her baby last night," she said with a sense of fresh excitement at imparting the news that stirred her so much. "Isn't that exciting?"

"It's about time," said Denny, gulping his orange juice with relish. "What's so exciting about babies? I don't want Shredded Wheat this morning. I was planning to eat Puffed Rice."

He carried the Shredded Wheat biscuit across the floor in his hand to put it into the box, sprinkling crumbs as he went.

"Denny!" Pat shrieked, all her sentiment about boys dissolved in irritation. "Carry it in the dish and don't spill crumbs."

He looked at her in genuine mystification. "What's wrong with crumbs?" he wanted to know. "I'll sweep them up."

He grabbed the broom and retrieved half a dozen wisps of Shredded Wheat while he scattered the rest along the edges of the counters, and Pat seized the broom in despair.

"You're supposed to collect the dirt, not spread it farther," she explained, demonstrating how to sweep the

171

dirt into a small pile, while Denny grinned at the success of his strategy.

"O.K., O.K.," he said, as if he had allowed her to do him a favor. Pouring milk on his cereal so fast that it spurted out of the dish onto the table, he settled down to eat it with his face six inches from the bowl, studiously absorbing the story on the back of the package as he ate.

Pat watched him in disgust, trying to reconcile her sentimental yearning for a baby boy with this real, live eleven-year-old, who was mostly a nuisance and not cute at all, as far as she, myopic with sisterly prejudice, could see.

Her parents came down, congratulated her on her breakfast, although the coffee was too weak Pat knew as soon as she poured out a cup for her mother. Pat ate her own breakfast, collected her books, and started toward the high school.

There she was back in her own environment again among contemporaries who were all interested in Connie's new status, but who obviously considered babies and family responsibilities as belonging to an older generation. Pat recognized that feeling as one of the elements that confused her: sometimes she wanted a baby, she wanted her own home, she was ready to settle down. But she did not yet feel like a member of the older generation.

The cloud bank of dreams kept separating and shredding apart, showing behind the dreams the solid blue of here and now, revealing as in a bright light all the happy excitement of being young and independent. It was a different kind of independence from that of adults: the giddy satisfactions of laughing with the girls, of walking slowly home in the soft pleasure of the early spring, eating the first ice-cream cone of the season, looking forward to more fun, more excitement, more independence in college. For the group who walked with Pat, adult life seemed too remote to worry about.

Nan was walking with them today, while her car was in the garage for lubrication, and she talked about all the things she wanted to do this summer and next year when she went far away to Europe or to college.

"What about Dick?" Pat asked.

Nan shrugged. "Oh, Dick can take care of himself. We're not going to go steady in college. It's better to be independent."

Independence was what Nan had. And Pat, who craved to be independent too in the sense of being released from parental influence, was not yet able to calculate the cost and determine that it was worth it.

She had talked all year about being independent enough to make her own decisions about Tim, and she had decided that she was going to marry him. But already she was no longer independent, because in almost every decision from now on she must consider him.

If she broke with Tim, she would no longer need to consider him. But would she be happy then? Obviously she would not. So that must not be the answer. She should be happy as she was now. But — a panicky feeling of never knowing how to choose and always making the wrong decisions swept over her, and she said hastily to Nan, to get away from her thoughts, "Is Dick coming to the performance of *Arsenic and Old Lace?*"

Nan laughed cheerfully. "Not Dick, my devoted sweetheart! He's got a chance to go out in the country that weekend with his uncle. You know, his uncle raises Arabian horses, and Dick spends a lot of time out there. So I said,

'Why don't you wait till another week when I could go along and ride some of those wonderful horses? And Dick said, 'Oh, you know me, Nan — I can't stand amateur plays!' "

"He sounds pretty choosy to me," said Pat. "Tim is coming down that weekend, because it's my birthday — so he'll come to the play."

"I don't care that much about Dick," said Nan. "He's handy when he's around, and when he isn't, there's always somebody else."

"Sometimes I wonder," said Pat, not sure whether she were being disloyal to Tim or only discussing her own doubts, "whether it's a good idea to go into college and be going steady with a boy."

"But I thought you weren't going steady with Tim this year," Nan said. "I thought that was settled last fall when he went away."

"We aren't, technically," Pat said, and some of the confusion was transparently, suddenly, clear. "The trouble is, I still feel as if we were. We can't either one of us feel happy about dating other people."

"What about the cast party? After all, you're one of the leads in this show," Nan reminded her. "Will you make him go to that?"

"I haven't decided whether I want to make him or not," Pat said.

"I wouldn't even consider going steady with anyone unless he would do what I wanted him to," said Lynn, tossing her blond head authoritatively. "In fact, I broke up with Mal over that very thing. He said he simply would not go to a horse show when I wanted him to. He wasn't interested in horses. And I said: 'Brother, this is it. If you

174

don't care enough about me to do what I want to do, I'll find someone who does.' I invited Randy to go, and we've been going steady ever since. Mal called and called, but I wouldn't take him back."

Perhaps, Pat thought, that was the difference between the way Lynn felt about boy friends and the way she felt about Tim. Lynn wanted to know that she could make a boy do anything for her, and Pat wanted to find a level of understanding where each could consider the other's needs and preferences.

"I don't know that I care that much about cast parties," she said. "I've been to two now, and they're all alike. If Tim doesn't want to go, I'd have more fun doing something else anyway."

"You could always go with Jack Willis," Nan reminded her. "After all, if Tim simply refused — and this is the show where you are one of the leads."

"I know," Pat agreed. "Oh, well — "

Uncertainty beset her again. It was all very well to hold high thoughts about considering each other and doing what the other would enjoy. But this cast party was going to be very special — she was one of the important people in the play — and the memory of Tim's discontent at the other party was still uncomfortable.

"I'll write him tonight," she planned half aloud. "I'll explain everything that is coming up that weekend, and he'll know what he's getting into."

She could not tell whether she was surrendering or winning in the battle with herself.

20

***

" Dear Tim:

" The weekend of my birthday is the production of *Arsenic and Old Lace* — the show where I have a lead, as I told you. This is a darling play, and I know you will like it."

Pat stopped writing and considered what she had written. She hoped he would like it.

" Anyway," she went on, " it's not Shakespeare, and of course the cast party afterward is going to be wonderful."

She stopped again.

She wanted to see him on her birthday. She was going to be eighteen, which meant that she was growing up, her most important birthday. At first it had seemed such a happy coincidence to celebrate that important occasion with her first lead in a high school play. She wanted Tim to see her in the play. And she wanted intensely to be a guest of honor at the party afterward and feel entirely unconfined in her enjoyment.

She held her head in her hands and thought about the party: some of the gang would be singing, as they always did; some of the others would be going over again the lines of the play just produced. She would be an important part of that happy reminiscence, recalling the successes, the near calamities, the flubs, the quick recoveries of each of three performances. That reminiscent reliving of excitement was almost as important as being part of the original experience. The teachers would be there, on the friendly joking basis with the students that they seemed to reach only at these parties. All her friends would be there, all these delightful people she had come to know in her senior year and enjoyed so much. And this was the last play of the year, the last year of high school life, the last time she could have this special, wonderful evening.

If she took Tim, he would be bored and her fun would be spoiled.

Slowly she tore up the letter she had written and started over again.

" *Dear Tim:*

" I've been counting on seeing you next weekend. But that is the night we are putting on *Arsenic and Old Lace,* and I'm going to the cast party afterward. I know how you feel about cast parties, and I don't want to make you go to this one."

She stalled again.

Suddenly without warning the aching loneliness swept over her. She could see Tim's wide grin, his dark eyes full of love, and something recalled to her that time last fall when they had felt so close and inseparable, that moment of understanding that was the most important achievement of love. She could see the anguish with which he would understand at once her meaning when she finished her letter with, " Why don't you come some other weekend? " He would be convinced that she no longer loved him.

But she did love him. That was what made the choice so difficult.

She sat there, her pen in her hand, picturing the coming weekend, moment by moment, if Tim did not come home.

The production of the play would be successful, she knew; the audience would be chuckling and occasionally howling, as the production staff had done through rehearsals. She hoped she would give a good performance. But Tim would not see it, so would it really matter? Afterward she would go on to the party with the crowd, and there she would drift about from one person to another, talking with this group and then with that one, listening to their laughter, perhaps with Jack Willis beside her. She would stay through the whole party, as she wanted to, coming home late, probably with Jack again. So she could do exactly as she wished. And after all, what would it mean?

She closed her eyes, wondering why she had to choose between two things dear to her heart when both were good. Her mother had said again and again, Pat remembered as if she had never understood it before: " Being in love means choosing one thing or another. It limits your choice. It means you must choose the most important thing, but you must be sure it *is* the most important."

The play was important; the party was important. But for Pat all the gaiety and celebration and triumph would be empty without Tim.

She wrote the letter again.

" *Tim, darling:*
" It will be so wonderful to see you next weekend. I have to be in this play that I wrote you about, but I think you'll

like it. I haven't decided whether I want to go to the cast party or not. We can talk that over when you get here. It's going to be a big weekend, and the most important part is your coming home.

" All my love, Pat."

The week went swiftly by, almost too fast for the cast to feel ready for the Friday night performance. The dress rehearsal on Thursday left everyone exhausted and hysterical because the flubs had been so ridiculous. The Friday night performance was smooth and good, although for Pat it still seemed like dress rehearsal, because her family and Tim were coming for the Saturday performance.

On Saturday morning she was assailed again with an uneasy question, Did she really want Tim to be part of her Saturday night program after all? She wondered why this uncertainty kept disturbing her occasionally, when most of the time she was so sure.

" How can you ever tell what you want? " she asked her mother, leaning her head on one hand at the kitchen table when she had finished her breakfast, and absent-mindedly lifting spoonfuls of sugar and letting them pour back into the bowl.

Her mother was washing dishes, and if she sensed the urgency in Pat's question, she gave no sign of awareness. She talked with her back to her daughter, rinsing plates from an earlier breakfast and setting them into the drain basket with more care than usual.

" Sometimes you can't," she said, as if she knew exactly what Pat meant. " Sometimes you have to try a choice and see how it works out, and if you can leave the door open to change your mind, it helps you to decide."

Pat sighed. " I'm so sure about Tim most of the time.

179

And then, suddenly, I wonder."

Her mother left the sink and poured a cup of coffee.

"You mean, whether you really want to give up some of the things you have to give up on Tim's account?"

"Exactly."

Mrs. Marlowe sat down at the table and thought awhile.

"When you choose love, you usually give up freedom," she suggested.

"But when I think about freedom without Tim that doesn't seem worth-while, either."

"That's part of the trouble with falling in love so young. You do give up a lot."

"But it's worth it," Pat defended her love with conviction.

Her mother smiled. "That's the whole question. I can't tell you whether it is or not. All I can point out is the problem. You have to find the answer for yourself; no one can tell you."

Pat got up restlessly and picked up a dish towel. As she finished drying the last cup the doorbell rang. Tim was home. The minute Pat saw him all her doubts dissolved.

"Hi, darling!" He was the same as he always had been, handsome, cheerful, delighted to be home again. "Isn't this wonderful?"

Held close in his arms, Pat knew that truly it was wonderful. At this moment she could not understand her doubts at all.

Spring was a delightful season to be in love, Pat thought, feeling as if she had never been aware of spring before. They strolled along the lake front in the late morning, watching the sun glittering on the changing water; they walked past the neighbors' lawns, looking at flower gardens, happy in being together.

"Now about tonight," she said, before he left her for dinner. "I'll see you after the performance. You're coming with the family."

"Isn't there a cast party?"

"Well, yes, there is. But I didn't know if you'd — I knew you wouldn't want to go to it, so I thought we'd do something else."

"I'd just as soon go," he said astonishingly. "It's your senior year, your last cast party. I wouldn't want you to miss it."

"Honestly?"

She wanted to hug him; she felt dissolved with love again. This was what made her love him so much, this knowledge that he knew what really mattered to her.

"But I thought you'd be bored, darling. I didn't want to make you spend your time doing something you didn't like."

"So what's the difference?" he wanted to know, with a little grin. "Look, here's the way I see it. I'd rather let you have fun and go along with you than keep you from it or not be with you. And someday you can do the same favor for me."

"Well, if you think you can stand it —" she was half delighted, half doubtful, still.

"It'll be fun to be with you," he assured her.

Tim was the first person to reach Pat when the final curtain was rung down, the final curtain call taken. She was still quivering with the excitement of success, glowing with pleasure and surrounded with friends who shared the success and the pleasure.

"Tim!" she cried, making her way through the tangle

181

of ropes, scenery, and backstage properties. " Oh, darling, I didn't expect to see you backstage! "

" When you're one of the stars, I have to join your fans," he teased.

" How did you really like it? I never had so much fun. Wasn't it wonderful? "

" Swell play," he said, still laughing over the closing scene. " I like that kind of thing. You were good, Pat. Very good. Better than I realized you were. How soon will you be ready to leave? "

" Oh, not yet! " she cried. " There are hundreds of people I want to see."

He regarded her, and his grin faded a little. She could see the thought cross his mind as if he had spoken it aloud: Pat is always the last to leave a crowd. He would always be waiting for Pat to say good-by to hundreds of friends before she would be ready to join him.

She waved and said: " I'll be out in a minute, honey. Really."

And because she knew he was waiting, she sped her farewells, told everyone she would see them at the party, and joined Tim with her family within ten minutes. Taking his arm, she announced gaily: " All ready to leave. We won't be late, Mother. We'll probably leave by one, if not sooner."

Tim cocked an eyebrow at her, but he said nothing, and they went out to the parking lot.

" We might even leave by twelve thirty," Pat said, as he opened the door for her to climb into Hortense. " The party doesn't mean that much to me. I'd rather have some time to be by ourselves when you're home."

He turned and held her close a minute.

"I brought you something," he muttered. "And then I couldn't decide about the best time to give it to you. Maybe I should have sent it up to the stage. Here."

He thrust a box into her hands, and she stared at it.

"A corsage? But Tim — it isn't a dance or anything —"

"Open it up," he encouraged her. "It's to celebrate a lot of things: your acting tonight, your last cast party, your eighteenth birthday tomorrow. And because I think you're worth it, and then some."

She opened the box and gazed enrapt at the most beautiful white orchid she had ever seen.

"But, Tim, it's gorgeous!" she cried, in complete astonishment. "My first orchid! Oh, you darling! What a wonderful time to get it!"

"Most girls," he said, when he had finished kissing her, "get them when everyone else gets them, like for the prom. That's when I don't think they're worth the money — because everyone is wearing them. But tonight I felt like giving you an orchid because tonight means so many special things."

He did understand how she felt about things, Pat thought, pinning the orchid on her spring jacket and feeling its white wings brush her cheek. This gesture from Tim meant more than it ever could from any other boy. If you could spend careless dollars on a whim, nothing meant very much. But when you must count your money as Tim must, then a gesture like this meant a very great deal. And suddenly all the luxury she had coveted this year fell into perspective and became unimportant.

Strangely, wearing a beautiful orchid made her feel entirely different from the way she had expected to feel. She had believed that to display such a token of wealth would

183

give her a sense of triumph that would raise her importance in her own eyes and in the eyes of everyone else.

Now she did not feel like that at all. She glanced down at
the orchid again. It was beautiful, it meant that Tim loved
her, and that was all that counted. She could not feel triumphant; she felt only a deeper love for Tim for the meaning this special gift conveyed. And she knew that some
eep hunger had been not assuaged but exorcised. If this
vere to be the only orchid in her life, it would be enough.
Now she must put this feeling into words.

"Darling, I love you more than ever," she said, almost
weeping with happiness.

Tim glanced down with a pleased grin as he swung off
the street to park in front of the house where the party was
already beginning.

"I love you too." He kissed her again.

"And now that I'll be eighteen in about two hours," she
said with a kind of awe that she had earlier had no time to
contemplate, "I'm grown up. Isn't that surprising, after all
this time?"

"Oh, I don't know," Tim laughed at her. "You've been
working your way up for a long time."

She sat up straight and turned toward him, her eyes
shining in the dark.

"Now that I'm old enough to do anything I want," she
said, "I've found out I'm grown up enough to wait. We can
take our time and have fun while we're waiting to get married. Don't you feel that way?"

"I found that out this spring," Tim said. "I knew it
would last and there was no big rush."

Pat opened her door, blissfully content, and the orchid
brushed her cheek again.

184

"I don't care how soon we get away from this mob," she said to Tim. "All of them together don't mean as much as you do. Let's run in and show them my orchid, and say hello and good-by."

And she meant exactly that.

Anne Emery was born Anne Eleanor McGuigan in Fargo, North Dakota. She has lived in Evanston, Illinois, since she was nine years old, and there attended Evanston Township High School and took a B.A. degree at Northwestern University.

Following her graduation, her father, a professor of pharmacology and therapeutics at the University of Illinois, took the family abroad for a year, where they visited his birthplace in northern Ireland and toured the British Isles, France, Switzerland, and Italy. She spent nine months studying at the University of Grenoble in France.

Upon return, Anne McGuigan taught in the Evanston schools, four years in the seventh and eighth grades at Haven Intermediate School, and, after her marriage in 1933 to John D. Emery, six more years in the fourth and fifth grades at Orrington School.

Then she retired from teaching to keep house and take care of her family. There are now five young Emerys: Mary, Kate, Joan, Robert, and Martha. Mary is in college this year, and Joan and Kate are in high school, so both the college and high school backgrounds of Mrs. Emery's stories are drawn from close-range observation.

187